PROBLEMS

The men led Chance to the van and bundled him into the back. The doors slammed shut behind them, then the van turned in a slow circle and drove out through the broken gates.

Jade and Rich waited a moment, then walked slowly after the van, out into the street. Neither of them spoke. And neither of them noticed the woman with long black hair who stood in a dark doorway farther along the street. Nor did they see the man in a long gray raincoat standing in the shadows outside the gates. But the woman did. She watched as the man took off his dark-framed glasses and wiped the rain from them with a crisply ironed white handkerchief. Then he waited until the twins were out of earshot before using his cell phone.

"Phillips here, sir," he said, as soon as his call was answered. "I came to meet Chance as arranged, but I'm afraid there's a bit of a problem." He watched the two children turn out of the end of the lane into the main street beyond. "Make that a couple of problems," he said gravely.

OTHER BOOKS YOU MAY ENJOY

Ark Angel	Anthony Horowitz
Hunted: Fake ID	Walter Sorrells
The Outsiders	S. E. Hinton
Payback	Andy McNab & Robert Rigby
Point Blank	Anthony Horowitz
Prep	Jake Coburn
Rooftop	Paul Volponi
Scorpia	Anthony Horowitz
Skeleton Key	Anthony Horowitz
Soldier X	Don Wulffson
Stormbreaker	Anthony Horowitz
Traitor	Andy McNab & Robert Rigby
The Unseen: It Begins	Richie Tankersley Cusick

JACK HIGGINS

WITH JUSTIN RICHARDS

SURE FIRE

speak

An Imprint of Penguin Group (USA) Inc.

SPEAK
Published by the Penguin Group
Penguin Group (USA) Inc., 345 Hudson Street, New York, New York 10014, U.S.A.
Penguin Group (Canada), 90 Eglinton Avenue East, Suite 700, Toronto, Ontario, Canada M4P 2Y3
(a division of Pearson Penguin Canada Inc.)
Penguin Books Ltd, 80 Strand, London WC2R 0RL, England
Penguin Ireland, 25 St Stephen's Green, Dublin 2, Ireland (a division of Penguin Books Ltd)
Penguin Group (Australia), 250 Camberwell Road, Camberwell, Victoria 3124, Australia
(a division of Pearson Australia Group Pty Ltd)
Penguin Books India Pvt Ltd, 11 Community Centre, Panchsheel Park, New Delhi - 110 017, India
Penguin Group (NZ), 67 Apollo Drive, Rosedale, North Shore 0632, New Zealand
(a division of Pearson New Zealand Ltd)
Penguin Books (South Africa) (Pty) Ltd, 24 Sturdee Avenue,
Rosebank, Johannesburg 2196, South Africa

Registered Offices: Penguin Books Ltd, 80 Strand, London WC2R 0RL, England

First published in Great Britain by HarperCollins Children's Books, 2006
First American edition published by G. P. Putnam's Sons,
a division of Penguin Young Readers Group, 2007
Published by Speak, an imprint of Penguin Group (USA) Inc., 2008

1 3 5 7 9 10 8 6 4 2

Copyright © Harry Patterson, 2006
All rights reserved

THE LIBRARY OF CONGRESS HAS CATALOGED THE G. P. PUTNAM'S SONS EDITION AS FOLLOWS:
Higgins, Jack, date.
Sure fire / by Jack Higgins with Justin Richards. — 1st American ed. p. cm.
Published in Great Britain in 2006 by HarperCollins Children's Books.
Summary: Resentful of having to go and live with their estranged father after the death of
their mother, fifteen-year-old twins Rich and Jade soon find they have more complicated
problems when their father is kidnapped and their attempts to rescue him involve them in
an extremely dangerous international plot to control the world's oil.
ISBN: 978-0-399-24784-2 (hc)
[1. Spies—Fiction. 2. Fathers—Fiction. 3. Twins—Fiction. 4. Brothers and sisters—
Fiction. 5. Adventure and adventurers—Fiction.] I. Richards, Justin. II. Title.
PZ7.H534954Sur 2007 [Fic]—dc22 2007008144

Speak ISBN 978-0-14-241213-8

Printed in the United States of America

Design by Katrina Damkoehler
Text set in Plantin

SURE FIRE

PROLOGUE

Two intruders moved through the oil storage depot, dark shapes against the black night.

One of them crept like a panther, silent and dangerous, leading the way through the jungle of pipes and cables, walkways and stairways. The other man had a limp and walked with the aid of a stick. Huge circular metal tanks rose up on either side of the two figures as they made their way toward their target.

"Jammer seems to be working," the man with the limp whispered, consulting a device strapped to his wrist like a watch. A small red light flashed rhythmically where the dial should have been.

His colleague nodded. His smile was barely visible in the black of the camouflage makeup that smeared his face. "No skimping on this job. Come on, they'll realize there's a problem if we hang around too long in one place."

The jammer scrambled the wireless connection between the cameras that were nearest to the intruders and the security control room on the other side of the complex. The effect would be to make the security monitors in the control room flicker on and off, seemingly at random.

The two men paused. The one with the stick pressed a button that turned off the jammer on his wrist. "No cameras in this area. We're in a blind spot. Should be safe for a minute."

The other man nodded his agreement. "Let's have a look at the map."

On the ground between them, they unfolded a detailed map of the complex. The man without the stick pulled something from the pocket of his black trousers: a pack of cigarettes and a lighter.

"You're joking!" the man with the stick said. "You can't light up here, John."

John smiled. "Might seriously damage my health, you think, Dex? I didn't bring a flashlight—this is to read the map."

"Yeah, well, I do worry about my health. And yours."

Dex produced a penlight and switched it on. "Now stop mucking about and put that lighter away."

The lighter glinted as John put it away. It flashed in the penlight's beam for a moment, an engraving on its side visible for a second—a simple outline of a heart.

"You always were the cautious one," John said.

"For all the good it did me," Dex muttered. "The one time I try it your way, and look what happens." He tapped his walking stick against his leg.

John didn't seem to notice. He was tracing a route on the map with his finger. "Looks easy enough. Turn the jammer back on. Let's do what we came for and get out of here."

The building they wanted was a boxy concrete block with no windows and a single metal door. A red security light cast its glow over the doorway, illuminating a uniformed guard standing outside. The shadow of a holster at the guard's side left the intruders no doubt that he was armed.

"Might as well put up a notice," John whispered. " 'Stuff worth stealing is in here.' Back in a moment." Like a ghost, he disappeared into the night.

Seconds later, a sound like a stone falling made the guard move from his post. He drew his gun and walked cautiously along the front of the building. From the opposite side, a dark shape moved quickly, creeping up behind him. The guard only knew of it when a handkerchief was clamped over his mouth.

John laid the sleeping guard on the ground in the shadows next to the building. He returned the handkerchief soaked in anesthetic to a small plastic bag and sealed it shut, before stuffing the bag back into his pocket. Dex knelt down awkwardly by the door and set to work picking the lock.

"Hold my stick, will you?" he asked. "And keep the light steady."

Red light spilled across the threshold to the inside as the door swung open. John helped his friend to his feet and gave him back his stick, then handed him a headset—infrared goggles attached to a set of straps that fit exactly over their heads and held the goggles tightly in position.

The view through the goggles was remarkably clear, and showed a large room crisscrossed with pipes that came in and out through the walls. A long narrow bench stood in the middle of the room, covered in glassware like a school science lab. Along one wall was advanced electronic equipment—computers, centrifuges and spectroscopic analyzers. Several drum-shaped canisters stood at the far end of the room—smaller versions of the huge oil tanks outside—linked together by narrow pipes, which then joined a larger pipeline that disappeared out through the side wall.

"You set the charge on the pipeline," John whispered, handing Dex a compact device. It looked like a plain black box with a small screen set in one side. "I'll get the sample."

Dex took the device and found the point where a number of the pipes converged. He set to work, attaching the device just below one of the valves where the thin pipe from the canisters joined.

Meanwhile, John was examining the canisters at the other end of the room. Carefully, he unscrewed the top of one of them and saw that it was filled with a pale, viscous liquid. He glanced over at the laboratory workbench for something to put the sample of the liquid into. There were test tubes and beakers and jars, but all were made of glass. His eyes wandered around the room, looking for anything that might be of use.

Set high in the corner of the walls, a video camera swung slowly toward him. A thin wire emerged from the camera and disappeared into the ceiling above. John stared at the tiny red light on top of the camera and the wire emerging from the back of it. The camera moved around until it was pointing straight at him.

"We've got a problem," John said. He grabbed the only container he could think of and reached into the open canister. "I think you should hurry."

The sirens started—a sudden, high-pitched wail of sound. Dex gave John a thumbs-up and they ran for the door. "That camera must be linked directly to the control room," Dex said. "So the jammer didn't work on it."

They could hear the footsteps and shouts of guards behind them.

Dex was limping badly now and John had to help him

along. "Leave me," Dex said. "I'm only slowing you down."

"I didn't leave you in Afghanistan and I'm not leaving you now. I'll throw you over the perimeter fence if I have to."

Searchlights snapped on. "They can't shoot," Dex gasped. "Not with all that fuel about."

Before John could answer, there was a loud crack from behind them, and a bullet ricocheted off the concrete pavement close to their feet.

"Maybe someone should tell them that," John said. "Come on!"

The security center was in chaos. Uniformed guards shouted into phones and radios. People hurried from monitor to monitor, working the cameras. Then the door swung open and a man entered. The room went quiet.

"Tell those idiots to stop shooting," the man said. He spoke with the trace of an Irish accent.

He did not speak loudly, but his words were clearly audible across the whole room. He was a short man, very thin, dressed in a simple dark sweater and jeans. His features were narrow and angular, and his hair was a gray crew cut. There was a distinctive scar under his left eye, faint white lines splaying out from it so the scar looked like a pale spider on the man's face.

"I want those intruders caught," the man ordered. "I

want to know what they were doing and who sent them. I want to talk to them before they die."

No one in the room doubted that the intruders would die—once the man got hold of them. His name was Ryan Stabb, but everyone called him by his last name. The name was short and brutal, like its owner.

"Why isn't that camera working?" Stabb demanded, pointing at a screen of static. As he spoke, the screen cleared.

"Don't know, sir," the guard at the main console said. "They keep cutting out, just for a few seconds. It always happens when there's a storm."

"There isn't a storm," Stabb pointed out. "But there will be if you don't get them. They must have a jammer. That's why the screens cut out." He leaned over the guard and jabbed a finger at one of the many monitors as it crackled to static. "That's where they are. You can trace them by the cameras that are affected. Work out where they're heading. And stop them."

The intruders heard the barking before they saw the dark shape of the dog emerge from the gloom. It bounded toward them, teeth glinting in the searchlights as it snapped its jaws in anticipation.

Dex swore, but John faced the dog and raised his arms. He gave a strange, high-pitched whistle. As he lowered his arms, the dog slowed. It stopped in front of John, panting heavily but no longer snapping. John stooped down beside the dog, reaching for its leather collar.

"Good boy!" John said. "I picked that up from an old Irishman who used to go to the same pub."

"Hurry up," Dex urged.

"All done," John assured him. "Aren't we, boy? Off you go." He ruffled the dog's fur and gestured for it to be on its way. The dog ran off into the darkness.

"Right then, back this way, I think." John headed back down the alley between several oil storage tanks.

"You're almost there," the guard said into the microphone. "Camera 11B just went. Looks like they're making for the south exit gate. That or the kennels." He turned to smile at Stabb. Stabb did not smile back. "They're going at quite a lick. Must be sprinting along," the guard said, turning back to the monitors.

"But they must know the main gates will be guarded," Stabb said. "What are they playing at?" He frowned at the control console as another monitor snowed across. "What were they doing in the lab? Has it been searched?"

"They got out of there straightaway, sir," another guard said. "No point searching for them there."

"Not for them," Stabb said. "I want to know what they were doing."

"Sabotage?" the guard asked.

"Search it," Stabb told him. "That's the only treated sample we have." He considered a moment before deciding. "Pump it out. Get it to another storage tank outside the lab. Just in case."

"Which tank, sir?"

"I don't care," Stabb said.

"Number three is empty and sterile," the guard said. "I can work out which valves need opening."

"Just do it," Stabb told him. "Do it now."

Farther down the room, the guard at the main monitors said with satisfaction into the microphone: "That's it. You've got them now. They're coming right to you!"

The security guards had their weapons leveled. They could hear something moving, coming toward them out of the glare of searchlights. Moving fast.

"Ready, lads?" the leader asked.

"Ready for anything," the man next to him said.

Then they both stared in astonishment as a shape appeared out of the glare and came toward them.

Following Stabb's orders, a valve inside the laboratory was opened remotely from the security control room. Fluid slowly started to flow from one of the canisters, along the pipe and toward the junction where the black box was attached.

A cold fluorescent light flickered on inside the room as the guards entered.

"What the hell's this?" a guard asked, bending to examine the black box.

"Don't touch," another warned.

"It's all right. Doesn't look like it's been primed."

"Anything could set it off. Remote trigger, change of temperature . . . Just be careful."

The guard leaned forward to remove the black box from the pipe.

"A dog?"

Stabb stared at the image on the monitor. A security guard was holding a large Alsatian dog by its collar. In his other hand, the man was holding what looked like a wristwatch.

"This was strapped to its paw. I've turned it off now."

Stabb said nothing. He was thinking. If the intruders were that clever, then they would have predicted every detail of how the guards would react. "Stop the flow," he shouted. "Close the valves on the sample canisters—now!"

The pale fluid in the laboratory reached the open valve that led into the main pipeline.

As it flowed through, a tiny circuit in the black box attached to the outside of the same pipe registered the distinctive vibration in the metal of the pipe—a vibration that could only be caused by the movement of fluid under pressure. The circuit sent a signal to another component in the box.

The guard leaped back as the readout blinked into life. It showed a number: 10.

"What the . . ." The guard's voice dried in his throat as 10 became 9.

Then he was running—grabbing his colleague by the arm and dragging him along toward the door.

8.

In a small service road outside the complex, a car was parked. It was a very ordinary car—unremarkable make, normal sort of model, nondescript color. Inside it were two extraordinary men.

John was smoking a cigarette. "We'll wait a moment," he said to Dex, who sat in the passenger seat. "Until they're distracted."

"Should be any second now, if they're on the case."

The whole security control center shook with the power of the explosion. Monitors flickered and died. Those that stayed on showed the fireball ripping through the heart of the installation, the ball of black smoke billowing into the air.

Stabb struggled to retain his balance as another larger explosion tore through one of the main tanks. Then another went up.

And another.

He gritted his teeth and scratched at the spider-like mark on his face. It itched like hell—as if his anger were about to erupt through the scar. That anger was not diminished in the slightest by the sight of a car on one of the monitors. It was driving slowly along one of the service roads, back toward the main road. It didn't have its headlights on, but the orange glow of the fire lit up the sky.

Stabb shoved aside the guard in front of the monitor and reached for the camera controls. The picture zoomed in—showing two dark figures silhouetted inside the car. There was yet another explosion as the whole complex caught fire, illuminating the car's license plate.

Smoke drifted across the picture, and the car was lost to sight.

1

Sandra Chance never saw the car that killed her. Just back from several years working in New York for a multinational computer company, she looked the wrong way as she stepped off the Manchester pavement. It was an easy mistake—she was so used to the traffic driving on the other side of the road. The driver was not to blame, but he didn't stop to find out.

The funeral was a quiet affair at the local church in the Manchester suburb she had moved to just a few weeks before. Though she was originally from the area, she had no family there—no family anywhere. Except the children.

Richard and Jade were just fifteen when their mother died. Twins, they had always shared everything—toys, games, books, arguments, and now grief. Rich typically kept things bottled up, but now the sadness was there. His eyes were welling with tears as he stood with his sister in the front pew.

Jade let the tears run freely down her cheeks as they listened to the priest's words about their mother—about their loss, their bravery and their devotion. Rich preferred to keep his emotions to himself, but Jade would know how he felt—she always knew how he felt—and that was all that mattered. He didn't care about anyone else. He didn't have anyone else now.

A few other locals had turned up, out of respect rather than love, but none of them had known Sandra Chance or her children. Mary Gilpin was the only person who knew her at all, as a neighbor and childhood friend. The twins were staying with her now, but Mary's husband, Phil, had never liked children, and had been quick to involve "the authorities." He hadn't even come to the church.

As the priest mentioned Mary Gilpin's name, she looked up. Jade glanced at her, smiled sadly and looked away again. Rich didn't react at all.

Then the door at the back of the church creaked open. The sound seemed even louder in the still moment of silence. Rich looked around. He stared at the man who stepped quietly into the church and closed the door behind him.

Rich watched the man cross himself and go to the nearest pew at the back of the church. He was a big man, but he moved quietly and easily. When he sat, there was a stillness about him, but also a contained strength. He looked about forty, with a rugged, experienced face and short blond hair. He was wearing a black suit and might have passed unnoticed and unremarked in a crowd except, Rich saw, for the man's eyes. They were bright blue—like Rich's own—and moved in a slow arc, as if he were taking in every detail of the church and people around him.

Jade had also turned and she too saw the man. The man's eyes met hers, just for a second, then moved on to Rich. The two children looked at each other and frowned. Jade squeezed her brother's hand. She flicked her head to get her hair out of her eyes, and they both knelt to pray.

The cold autumn sun was low in the sky, casting long shadows of the tombstones across the churchyard. Jade and Rich stood together a little way from the grave.

"She should have looked the right way," Jade said. Like her brother, she had a trace of American accent—not much, but enough for people to notice. "She was always warning us, telling us to be careful. Not to be in too much of a rush."

"Don't blame her," Rich told her.

"I'm not," Jade protested. "It's just . . . " She sniffed and looked away. "She should have looked."

The man from the back of the church was talking to the priest and Mrs. Gilpin. There was another woman with them, a middle-aged woman with obviously dyed hair. Rich knew she was with Social Services. She was supposed to be looking after him and Jade until someone decided what to do with them. He couldn't remember her name and he didn't care.

"Who is that man?" Jade said. "I feel like I've seen him somewhere before."

Rich shrugged. "More Social Services."

"Why are they here?" Jade said.

"We can't stay with the Gilpins forever."

Jade stared at him, her tearstained face framed by her long blond hair.

Rich sighed and went on: "Didn't you hear Mr. Gilpin last night, going on at her again about how she can't be expected to look after us and it isn't fair on him?"

"Maybe we can go back to New York," Jade said. "Stay with Charmaine and her family."

"Yeah, right," Rich muttered. "Like one of your old school friends is going to take us both in." He could sense Jade glaring at him, and looked away.

The woman from Social Services was shaking the strange man's hand. She glanced over at Rich and Jade, then walked quickly away. The man seemed to gather himself, squaring his shoulders and taking a deep breath that made his chest heave. Then he and Mrs. Gilpin came over to where the twins were standing.

"Hello," the man said. His voice was deep and rich, and he tried to smile. He reached his hand out toward Rich, such a natural gesture that Rich found himself taking the man's hand and shaking it. The man's grip was firm and confident.

Rich felt his insides turn to water as the man introduced himself.

"John Chance," he said. "I'm your father."

2

The twins sat at the back of the church with John Chance while the priest tidied things away and worked in the vestry.

"How can you be our dad?" Jade demanded as soon as they sat down.

"Why should we believe you?" Rich asked.

"It's as much of a shock for me too," Chance said.

"Why didn't Mum say anything?" Jade asked. "We didn't even know she'd been married."

"It was a long time ago," Chance said. "Sixteen years. I

came home one day and she was gone. She left a note, but it didn't say much. I assumed I'd hear—from her lawyers if not from Sandy herself."

"No one called her Sandy," Jade snapped. "Mum hated it."

"I'm sorry," Chance said. "Until last week I really didn't know anything. Then I got a call from Mrs. Gilpin. Apparently, your mother left a letter with her—in case anything happened to her."

Chance smiled, but it looked strained. "I did love your mother very much," he said. "I believed she loved me."

"Believed?" Jade prompted.

Chance turned away. "She never asked for a divorce—she even carried on using my name. We're still married." He hesitated, realizing his mistake. "*Were* still married. That's partly why you're in my care."

"I'm sorry if it's spoiled your day," Jade said sharply.

"That isn't what I meant," he said.

"I guess it's a shock for you too," Rich said. He put his hand on Jade's shoulder for comfort. She put her hand over the top of it. No matter what else happened, they always had each other.

"Just a bit," Chance confessed. "But, look—we'll make it work. I'm in the middle of some business right now, quite intense stuff. But that should be over soon. By the end of term, when you come home, we'll be able to spend some time and sort out where we go from here, okay?"

"Come home?" Rich echoed. "You mean we're staying up here till the end of school?"

"With the Gilpins?" Jade asked. "While you go back to London?"

Chance looked awkward. "Not exactly. That isn't what I meant."

"Then what did you mean, *Dad*?" Jade asked sarcastically.

"Look, I haven't exactly had time to plan this," Chance told them. "I live in a tiny flat right now. It's hardly big enough for me, let alone the three of us. And I'm working all the hours God sends. I can't get you to and from school and cook your meals and look after you and—"

"And change our diapers?" Jade said. "We're fifteen. We can cope. Mum worked, you know."

"We'll discuss it at the end of term, all right?" Chance said.

"And where will we be in the meantime?" Rich wanted to know.

But Jade was staring openmouthed at Chance. "No way. Absolutely no way at all, ever, on this earth." She looked over at Rich.

And he realized what she had already guessed. "Boarding school is right out," he agreed. "Not if it's the last school on the planet."

"Just till the end of this term," Chance told them. "Till I can spend some time with you and work this out."

"No way," Jade said.

"Never," Rich told him.

Chance stood up. His voice was quiet, but they could both sense an undercurrent of determination. "I'm not asking you. I'm your father and I have to decide. I'm sorry, but that's how it has to work. End of debate."

"That wasn't a debate," Rich said. "A debate involves two points of view and a decision based on the arguments. That didn't happen."

"You just decided for us," Jade added. "You've only just met us and already you can't wait to get rid of us."

"I'm not talking about it," Chance said. "Because you're right—there is no debate. It's decided."

"Oh—so suddenly you know what's best for us?" Jade said. She stood up and glared at Chance. "You abandon us and Mum sixteen years ago and now you're back and you know best? I don't think so."

"Wait a minute," Rich said. "Sixteen years ago. We weren't even born then."

"You didn't even wait till we were born?" Jade's eyes were watering as she spoke.

"Now hold on. Sandy—Sandra," Chance corrected himself quickly, "left *me*. It wasn't my decision. I'd never have left her. Even if . . ." He stopped abruptly.

"Even if what?" Rich asked.

Chance took a deep breath. "Look—until yesterday, I didn't know where your mother had gone, what she'd been doing. Until yesterday, I didn't know I was a father."

• • •

No one spoke all the way to the Gilpins' house. Chance parked the car in a space outside the house next door—the rented house that Rich and Jade had lived in for the last few weeks with their mother. Jade doubted he even realized that was their house.

"Everything's going into storage," Chance explained. "We can sort through all your stuff later, decide what you want."

"At the end of school term, right?" Jade sneered.

Mr. Gilpin answered the door. He shook hands with Chance and muttered something about condolences. He glared at Rich and ignored Jade. He stepped inside and gestured for them to come into the hallway.

Several boxes and shopping bags were lined up against the wall. Jade could see her own clothes spilling out of one of the bags. Schoolbooks shoved in a box. Rich's best sneakers in another.

"We could have packed our own stuff," she said.

Mr. Gilpin looked away. "Thought you'd be in a hurry to be off."

"Someone's in a hurry all right," Jade said.

"We'd like to say good-bye to Mrs. Gilpin," Rich said. "We didn't really get a chance at the church."

Mr. Gilpin turned away. "She's not here. Gone out. Shut the door behind you."

Chance lifted one of the boxes. "I think we'd best be going," he said.

As they drove away, Jade watched the net curtains of the front room twitch.

Rich sat in the front and Jade sat in the back of the car.

Jade could see that Chance had angled the mirror so he could watch her.

Was he keeping an eye on her? she wondered. Was he expecting trouble from her?

She looked away, out the window. That was *his* problem, she decided. If he wanted trouble, he could have it.

She glanced at Chance again in the mirror, but he was looking straight ahead at the road. She studied his face—the line of his jaw, the way his nose sloped just like Rich's—just like her own. What did Chance think? What did he see beyond two fair-haired twins? Maybe—just maybe—he really did want to get to know the children he had never seen before.

"So, tell me about yourselves," Chance said, trying to be cheerful. "What do you like to do with your time?"

"Get driven about in cars that go too fast," Jade retorted.

Chance's laugh sounded strained, but he eased off the speed slightly. "Right. Anything else?"

Jade slumped back in the seat, looking out the window. She watched as their car overtook others. Soon they were going just as fast as before.

He hadn't listened to her, she decided. Nobody ever listened to her.

"I like reading," Rich was saying. "I read anything, but mostly I like to find out about stuff. How things work. That sort of thing. TV's good too. Hey," he thought suddenly, "do you have a PlayStation?"

"Sorry. Got a DVD player and a laptop. That's about it. What about you, Jade?"

She continued to stare out the window. "I like doing things, not reading about them. Is there a gym near you?"

"I've no idea."

"Figures."

Chance laughed again, only this time it sounded more genuine. "I keep pretty fit, you know."

"You think," Jade muttered.

"And my hearing's fine," he said. "You into that fitness stuff then?"

"A bit."

"And then some," Rich said. "She works out. Runs. She eats a lot of fruit and vegetables. Drinks loads of bottled water."

"It's good for you," Jade protested. "You have to look after yourself. Healthy body, healthy mind."

"Quite right," Chance agreed.

"Don't patronize me," she told him.

"I was agreeing with you."

"Well, don't."

"You'd rather I disagreed with you?" he asked.

"I'd rather you stopped pretending," Jade replied. She folded her arms.

They lapsed into silence.

Jade stared out the window and Rich turned his head to whisper to her over his shoulder. "It'll be okay," he told her. "We'll get through this; it won't be so bad. I mean, what's the worst that can happen? Apart from boarding school?"

"I just want Mum back," Jade said, her eyes filling with tears once again.

Chance was fumbling in his pockets as he drove fast and confidently down the outside lane. He pulled something out and Jade's expression changed at once—first to surprise and then anger.

Chance was trying to shake a cigarette out of a pack. He caught a glimpse of Jade's face in the rearview mirror.

"I'm gasping for a smoke," he told her.

Jade wiped her eyes and glared at him.

Chance put the cigarettes back into his pocket.

3

It was dark by the time they reached Chance's flat. It was on the second floor of a Victorian terraced house. The outside looked grim and dilapidated. Paint was peeling from the window frames by the door, and the stone steps were chipped and stained.

But once inside it was very different. There was a small elevator at the end of a wide hallway and a staircase wound up around the elevator shaft. Chance heaved open the heavy metal grille door across the elevator.

"Leave that open and it won't move," he explained. "Gives us time to put all your luggage inside."

They piled the boxes and bags inside, almost filling the floor space in the small elevator. Chance reached in through the door to press the button for the second floor, then he heaved the grille across again—leaving the three of them outside. The elevator started to move.

"We could have squeezed inside," Rich protested.

"But Jade wants us to keep fit," Chance said. "Come on—we have to get there before the elevator." He took the stairs two at a time with practiced ease.

"He'll be wheezing before he gets there," Jade said, running up the stairs. Rich sighed and followed at a more leisurely pace.

They dumped the last load of stuff into the hallway of Chance's flat. Chance himself had disappeared inside already. "Was he wheezing?" Rich asked.

"Expect so," Jade said. "Didn't notice."

"That's a 'no' then," Rich said.

There were three doors from the hallway. The first door led into the kitchen, the next into a living room. At the end of the hall was a small bathroom. Chance appeared from the kitchen and led the twins through to the living room. It looked like a show home—hardly any furniture, just a sofa and a low coffee table. A television and DVD player stood against one wall, beside an old fireplace, but there were no magazines or books or ornaments. The room was painted a uniform white that made it seem even more impersonal. The only sign of life was the ashtray on the coffee table—full of cigarette butts. It gave the room a stale, unpleasant smell. A single picture hung on the wall opposite the door. It showed a steam train speeding through the countryside—a sleek blue engine with a sloping front. In the foreground was a pond with ducks swimming on it.

"That's clever," Rich told Jade, pointing at the picture.

"Why?"

"Because the engine is called *Mallard*."

She shook her head, none the wiser.

"Mallard is a sort of duck," Chance said, joining them.

"Where's my room?" Jade demanded.

He pointed. "Through there, on the right."

"And mine?" Rich asked.

"Same place. Same room."

"You're kidding," Jade said. "We don't share. We're fifteen."

"There are only two bedrooms," Chance told her.

"Why can't Rich share with you?" Jade asked. "Boys together?"

Chance shook his head. "Because I'm sleeping on the sofa in here and there's only room on it for one. There are a couple of single beds in there."

"You said there were two bedrooms," Rich reminded him.

"I'm using the other one as a study. I have to work. You get a bedroom and beds; I get a study and the sofa. That's the best deal I can give you."

"That's no deal," Jade said.

"A deal is something that's agreed between two or more parties," Rich pointed out.

"And do you know what a smart aleck is?" Chance asked.

"Yes, I do, actually. It's—"

"I know what it is," Chance told him.

"Then why did you ask?" Rich asked.

"Dad's little joke," Jade told him. She shot a glance at Chance. "Very little joke. Come on." She led Rich through to the bedroom.

The room was bare apart from two single beds, two bedside cabinets and a mirror on one wall.

"No place like home," Jade said.

"And this is certainly no place like home," Rich agreed. "Let's get our stuff. We must have some posters or something to liven the place up."

The room that Chance was using as a study was opposite their bedroom. Jade pushed the door open and they looked inside. It was a contrast to the rest of the flat.

There was a single desk with a chair beside it. On the desk was an open laptop computer and a telephone. The rest of the desk was covered in piles of paper that extended to the floor and against the walls—piles of magazines and books. A bookshelf strained under the weight of files and heavy books.

"Oil industry stuff," Rich said, glancing at some of the titles. "Did he tell us he worked in the oil industry?"

"He's hardly told us anything," Jade said. She walked over to the desk.

"We shouldn't really be here," Rich said, following hesitantly.

"You're telling me." She pointed to a small box attached to the telephone wire. It was about the size of a pack of cigarettes, plain gray plastic with several buttons on one side. "What's that? A modem?"

"Don't think so," Rich said. "Weird-looking thing."

"I know what this is, though," Jade announced, grabbing a sheet of paper from beside the phone. "Look—a list of schools. Boarding schools, I bet. He's been crossing them off. God, he's already trying to get rid of us."

"What are you doing in here?" Chance asked. He was standing at the door to the study.

"Just having a look around," Jade said.

"Look—I think we have to have certain rules around here, and one of them is that you never come into my study."

"But we're your kids!" she protested.

"I'm sorry, but those are the rules," he said. He put his arm out, gesturing for them to leave the room.

"Come on," Rich said. He took the sheet of paper from

his sister and put it back on the desk. He glanced down the two columns of names—some of the schools he recognized. "There are two lists here," he said.

"What do you mean?" Jade asked.

"Come on now," Chance said.

"Two lists," Rich repeated. "As in two sets of boarding schools. As in boys' schools and girls' schools."

"No way! Oh, no way on earth," Jade yelled.

"You're not splitting us up," Rich agreed. He turned to face his father, his voice quiet but angry. "Jade and me—we've got nothing except each other. You're not taking that from us too."

Rich was slumped on the sofa, watching TV. It was a cartoon and he wasn't interested, but it was better than listening to Chance, who was sitting on the floor talking to him.

"I tried mixed schools first. Of course I did. But none of them had two spaces in the same year group."

"So you just thought you'd split us up," Rich said.

"What was I supposed to do?" Chance asked.

Rich said nothing. He turned up the volume of the television.

But he still heard Jade's shout from the kitchen, where she'd gone to empty the ashtray into the trash can: "What is this? You are one seriously weird guy."

Rich clicked off the TV and followed Chance to the

kitchen. Jade had the fridge door open and was unloading its contents onto the countertop. Bottles of beer.

"Is that all there is?" Rich asked.

"No. There's this too." She pulled out two bigger bottles and put those with the beer. Champagne. "I mean, where's the butter? Milk? Eggs? Food of any sort? Anything at all, really?"

"It's down the road," Chance said. He gently eased Jade to one side and started to repack the fridge.

"What do you mean, down the road?" she demanded.

"I get takeout or I eat at the pub. They're down the road."

"And that's how you live?" Jade was aghast. "No wonder the kitchen's so clean. At least you do the washing up."

"Eat out of the cartons usually," Chance said casually. He turned and winked at Rich, who stifled a smile.

"You are so gross," Jade told him. "Just don't expect us to sink to your level."

Chance shrugged.

"What about Chinese food for dinner?" Rich asked.

They ate take-out Chinese with the TV on. It meant they didn't have to talk to one another. Jade went to bed almost as soon as she'd finished her fried rice and spring roll. Rich pushed his sweet-and-sour chicken around the plate for a while, not really hungry.

"I'm tired," he said awkwardly. "I think I'll get to bed too."

"That's okay," Chance said. "I've got work to do anyway. Some calls to make. Don't worry—I'll tidy up."

Rich gave a weak smile and headed for the bedroom.

Jade was already in bed. She hadn't turned the light out and she was just staring at the ceiling. She frowned at Rich as he came in.

"Hey," he said.

She turned over, facing away.

"What's the matter?" he asked. "I haven't done anything."

She pulled the pillow over her head, not listening. So Rich pulled her duvet away.

"Give that back!" Jade was out of bed at once, grabbing the duvet. Rich let it go and went for her pillow instead. They faced each other, each brandishing bedding.

"Peace?" Rich suggested.

"If you give me my pillow back."

"Fair enough." He threw it to her.

Jade dropped the duvet and caught the pillow. Then she started hitting Rich with it, driving him back onto his bed.

"Hey, hey, hey!" He tried to fend her off.

"That's for ganging up on me," she told him.

"We're not—I wasn't. When?"

"In the kitchen. Getting Chinese."

"Yeah, as opposed to what?" Rich said. "There's no food in this house. Just beer, champagne and cigarettes. Which did you want for dinner?"

Jade flopped down on her bed, dragging the duvet back up over herself. "I'm sorry. It's all just so . . . sudden. So unfair."

She started crying again. Rich sat beside her on the bed.

"It is a nightmare," Rich agreed. He looked over at the bedroom door. "*He's* a nightmare. Maybe boarding school will be better."

"Oh, look," Jade said, sniffing between her tears. "Out the window."

The curtains were drawn and Rich frowned. "What?"

"Thought I saw a flying pig," Jade said.

4

In Krejikistan, the cut glass of a chandelier glittered as the light reflected off its facets. Electric bulbs had replaced the candles that once provided the light, but the ceiling above it still retained an original mural—a pale blue sky with delicate clouds drifting across.

The room below was enormous, with a floor made up of black and white marble squares. The space was made to seem even bigger by large mirrors that hung on the walls. The furniture—a highly polished wooden table that had been made for Louis XIV of France, high-backed chairs patterned in gold leaf that had been a gift to a tsar, and a series of seventeenth-century side tables—were almost lost in the huge space.

Viktor Vishinsky sat in one of the antique chairs. In front of him was a single place setting for dinner—heavy silver cutlery, an ornate bowl filled with stuffed olives and a glass of white wine. He was looking intently at a large screen that his technicians had set up at the other end of the table. The image was grainy and unclear.

"Is that the best you can do?" he asked. He took one of the olives from the bowl in front of him and rolled it between his finger and thumb.

"We have enhanced it as much as possible," Pavlov, the chief technician, assured him.

Vishinsky settled back in his chair and let them explain. To him, the images still looked crude and fuzzy. He pushed the olive into his mouth.

"You can see where the man at the back of the laboratory is opening the canister," Pavlov said. He froze the image. It was projected from a laptop computer onto the large screen. The high-tech setup looked out of place in the tsarist splendor of the huge room.

Two other technicians were standing nervously at the side of the room. Whether they were there in case Pavlov needed their own specialist expertise, or simply to give him moral support, Vishinsky did not know or care. His whole attention was focused on the speckled images on the screen.

Pavlov used a laser pointer and ran the red dot of light around the figure just visible by the shadowy shape of the canisters. "If we had images from an infrared camera—" he began.

But Vishinsky cut him off. "We do not. We must work with what we have. What can you tell me, apart from the obvious?"

Pavlov let the video run on. "As you can see, just, he is reaching inside the canister. As his hand comes out—there." He froze the video again and indicated the man's hand with the pointer. "He is holding something. Something which we must assume he dipped into the fluid and filled. It is not very big. We can tell from his hand that it is about the size of an eggcup." Pavlov paused for a moment, before adding, "It is not an eggcup, I should point out."

"I said omit the obvious. Is it something he found in the lab?" Vishinsky asked, taking another olive. "Or is it something he brought with him?"

"We can find no indication that any container of that size was in the lab. Unfortunately, there is nothing left of the lab, so it is impossible to be sure if anything was taken. But earlier in the sequence we see the man looking around, we think for a container. He finds nothing useful, so uses whatever he brought with him. See, here . . ." He wound the footage back at high speed before letting it play again. "He seems to take something from his pocket."

"Something that he had in his pocket," Vishinsky said.

"He may have come prepared, and then looked to see if

there was a more suitable or larger container to be found in the lab."

"But there was not."

Pavlov nodded. "All sterile glassware. Fragile, if you have to make a hurried escape."

The video was running forward again, at normal speed.

"There!" Vishinsky said suddenly. He leaned forward. "Go back—slowly."

Pavlov let the images play backward at a tenth of their normal speed. He froze the playback as soon as Vishinsky said, "Stop it there."

Vishinsky got up from his chair and walked slowly along the length of the table. His eyes never left the screen. The image showed the dark figure as his hand emerged from his pocket. The fingers were wrapped around whatever he was holding—the receptacle he was about to fill with liquid from the canister. In that single frozen frame, it was angled so that it caught what little light there was—perhaps a faint glow from the display of nearby equipment.

Vishinsky stood close to the screen. "Close in on his hand, on the thing he is holding."

Pavlov moved his fingers carefully across the laptop's track pad and the image zoomed in on the container in the man's hand.

Just barely visible was a shadow or a mark. Something on the container that was catching the light. "What is that?"

"I'm not sure." Pavlov tried to trace the mark with his

pointer, but it was not distinct enough. "A maker's mark perhaps? Maybe it's just a shadow, a reflection—an artefact of the enhancement process."

Vishinsky nodded. "Find out," he said.

"But, sir," Pavlov said, "we have already enhanced the image as much as we can. Any more and we risk introducing things that are not actually there." He hesitated and licked his dry lips.

"Don't trouble me with details," Vishinsky said. "Just find out what that mark is. You can do that, can't you? For me?"

He raised a gray-white eyebrow as if asking a simple favor of a friend.

Pavlov swallowed. "Of course, sir. We'll do what we can. But—"

"Find out!" Vishinsky roared. He waved his hand in sudden, abrupt dismissal and Pavlov quickly disconnected his laptop and hurried after his colleagues from the room. "And tell someone to bring me my food," Vishinsky said. "Before it gets cold."

5

The sound of a telephone woke Rich in the middle of the night. Instinctively, he fumbled for his cell, but it wasn't the same ring. He and Jade both had cell phones, though Mum had made them pay their own usage fees. Probably he was out of minutes anyway.

The phone stopped and, now that he was awake, Rich could hear the low sound of Chance speaking. Rich's cell phone showed the time as 04:32 A.M. Who was calling at half past four in the morning?

He needed the toilet now that he was awake, so he

tiptoed to the door and opened it. He paused. Chance's voice was muffled and indistinct through his closed study door, but Rich couldn't help catching a few words when he pressed his ear to the door.

". . . No, not here . . . better not meet yet . . . dangerous . . . leave it for me . . . usual place . . . I'll collect . . . soon."

The sound of Chance's voice stopped. If Chance had to be somewhere soon, he'd be in a rush, Rich realized. He darted back into his bedroom and pushed the door almost closed. The study door opened and through the crack between the door and its frame, Rich saw Chance hurry into the living room. He was still dressed.

Maybe he slept in his clothes, Rich thought. Maybe he didn't sleep at all.

Rich climbed back into bed, his need for the bathroom forgotten. When he woke again it was morning, and the events of the night seemed as vague as a dream.

Jade appeared in the bedroom door. She was still in her pajamas and carrying two mugs of tea. "He's gone," she said.

Rich told her about the nighttime phone call while they drank their tea. They went through to the study, where the computer was on. It showed a standard screen saver and there was a password prompt to get out of it and back to the main screen.

"Who needs a password when he lives alone?" Jade wondered.

"Maybe it's for our benefit," Rich said. "Or maybe

he takes the laptop to work. Maybe he's gone to work already."

"It's not seven o'clock yet," Jade pointed out.

"Long commute?"

"Or a long meeting. I wonder who called him."

"Let's find out," Rich said, lifting the phone. "1471—gives the number of the last caller."

"Probably withheld or unavailable," Jade said.

Rich tried it anyway. The dial tone was replaced by the beep of the buttons as he pressed them. But then, instead of a voice, he heard an electronic screech. It was so loud and shrill that Rich dropped the phone.

Jade could hear it too. She picked up the handset to replace it in the cradle. But then she hesitated, pointing at the plastic box attached to the phone. Lights were flashing on the side of it. She hung up and the lights went out.

"I don't like this," Jade said quietly.

Before Rich could reply, they heard the sound of the door to the flat slamming shut. They rushed to the living room.

Chance looked tired. He was holding a few letters, which he dropped unopened into the kitchen trash can. He closed up the cupboard where the bin was kept and turned the kettle on.

"Lucky we got milk with the Chinese food," Rich said from the doorway.

"I drink my coffee black," Chance replied, without looking around. "You're up early."

"We all are," Jade said, pushing past Rich into the kitchen. "Where have you been?"

"Couldn't sleep. Went for a walk."

The kettle was boiling and Chance made his coffee. "I've got some work to catch up on. I'll see you later. Help yourselves to breakfast."

"I guess he means the beer," Jade said, when Chance had gone into the study. "Unless there's some cereal hidden away." She opened a few cupboards, but found nothing. Having tried all the others, she opened the cupboard under the sink. This was the cupboard with the trash can. As the door opened, it raised the lid of the bin inside.

"Hang on—look at this." Jade was staring into the bin.

Rich joined her and saw what she was looking at—the letters that Chance had just dropped.

Rich lifted out the letters. "They're all the same," he said, showing her. There were five letters—bills and junk mail. The address was the same on them all—Second Floor Flat—and the number and street. And they had all been sent to the same person.

But that person wasn't John Chance. It was Harry Lessiter.

"Remind me," Jade said quietly. "How do we know that this man who says he's called John Chance but gets someone else's mail, who gets phone calls in the middle of the night and goes to 'meetings' until dawn—"

"How do we know," Rich finished for her, "that he's actually our John Chance at all?"

Chance told them he was working from home that day. He was more than happy for Jade and Rich to explore the area, and so the twins left him to his work and went to the shops. For lunch they got a sandwich in a little Internet café, and Rich spent an hour mucking about on the Web. Jade e-mailed her friend Charmaine in New York.

They found a small supermarket within easy walking distance and Jade bought bottled water, grapes, oranges and a spray air freshener. Rich bought potato chips and Coke. They thought about getting some food for the evening, but neither of them wanted to cook and they doubted Chance would offer. So they grabbed a few frozen meals to microwave.

When they got back, Chance was in the living room, talking on his cell phone. He hung up as soon as Rich and Jade came in. They exchanged glances, sure it was for their benefit.

"Can I ring my friend Charmaine?" Jade asked.

"Of course you can," Chance said. "You've got a cell phone."

"I'm almost out of credit."

"Me too," Rich said.

"Give me your cell numbers and I'll sort them out for you."

"I'll write them down for you later," Rich said.

"Just tell me. I'll remember. I'm good with numbers." He smiled. "Really."

Rich reeled off his cell number. Grudgingly, Jade told him hers too. Chance recited them both back perfectly.

"Charmaine's in New York," Jade said, as Chance offered his own phone. "It'll cost a fortune on that."

"There's the phone in the study," Rich suggested.

"Maybe later," Chance said.

"I need to call her now, before she leaves for school. You know—the time difference?"

Chance sighed. "All right, all right."

Jade didn't wait for more, but headed straight for the study. Chance hurried after her and Rich followed.

"Hang on," Chance said. "I need to set this up." He fiddled with the plastic box attached to the phone wire.

"What's that for?" Rich asked.

"Oh, it's . . . it's a security thing. Like a phone lock."

"There's only you here," Jade said. "Or was," she added.

"The company insists. I deal with a lot of sensitive stuff in my job."

"Like what?" Rich asked.

"Like I can't tell you." He finished working on the box. "That should work now. I'll leave you to it."

Rich followed him out. "Why did you throw your letters away?" he asked. "Junk mail?"

"Probably," Chance said. "Why do you ask?"

"Just curious."

"They were for the previous tenant of the flat. He didn't leave a forwarding address."

Rich nodded. "And no one writes to you?"

Chance smiled. "That's me—Johnny No-Mates."

The phone worked fine now, but Jade just got voice mail at Charmaine's house, so she rang Mrs. Gilpin instead.

Mrs. Gilpin seemed pleased to hear from her. "How is everything?" she asked.

"Oh, fine," Jade lied. "There's some shops nearby and a little park. And . . . Dad is sorting out school for us. We'll be okay."

"You must come back and visit us."

"Thank you. We'd like that." There was something funny with the phone—probably something to do with the plastic box. Jade could hear a clicking every now and again. But she thought nothing of it.

Three streets away from where Jade was making her phone call, an unmarked black van was parked on a side road.

Inside the van, a man wearing dark-framed glasses and a long gray raincoat was sitting in front of a sophisticated audio monitoring system. He wore headphones, listening intently to every word Jade said.

6

At Heathrow, Stabb was meeting a woman who had just arrived on a scheduled flight. As they walked to the short-term parking lot, Stabb told the woman how things were going.

"So you've achieved nothing," the woman said with a smile. She was beautiful, with long, straight, jet-black hair.

"It is difficult until we can get back the sample," Stabb said. "We can't risk losing that, and Chance could have hidden it anywhere. The only way to be sure is to get to

Chance as he hands it over. He must still have it, or there would have been some fallout by now."

"I agree. And so does Viktor."

Stabb scowled. "Glad to hear you both approve."

"Oh, don't misunderstand me," she said, smiling. She brushed her hair away from her face as she got into the car. "You are in charge here."

Stabb looked at her, then started the engine and pulled out of the parking space.

"So what do you want me to do?" she asked.

"Nothing for now. We're watching Chance, and so far he's not made contact with anyone. But the children may provide an opportunity."

The woman smiled, watching through the car window as a huge 747 took off into the cloudy sky. "I like children," she said.

"Jade won't like that," Rich warned Chance.

Chance lit the cigarette anyway. He put the pack and his silver lighter down on the coffee table beside his cell phone.

Chance blew out a long breath of smoke and Rich winced, trying not to cough. He hated the smell of cigarettes, hated the way the smoke got into your mouth and the stale smell of it lingered on your clothes.

"I've had a really long day," Chance said.

At that moment, Jade appeared in the doorway to the

living room. Rich recognized the expression on Jade's face and from experience he knew it was not good news.

She walked over to Chance and plucked the cigarette from his mouth. Then she ground it out in the ashtray.

"What are you doing?" Chance demanded.

"You're not smoking that," Jade told him.

"You can't order me about in my own flat."

"It might be your flat," Jade said, "but we all have to live here."

"Sometimes I just have to have one." He opened the cigarette pack again.

"You're killing us as well as yourself," Jade told him. "Killing your own children."

Chance was on his feet. He pushed the lighter into the space inside the cigarette pack, then closed the pack and tossed it down onto the table beside his phone. "I'm sorry, but I can't deal with this right now. I'll phone schools and you should be somewhere more pleasant by the weekend. Things are not easy for me at the moment—not easy at all."

He turned and walked quickly from the room.

As soon as the study door slammed shut, Jade scooped up the cigarettes from the coffee table. "Confiscated," she said. "Since we're all treating each other like schoolkids here. And that," she added, picking up Chance's cell phone. "That's confiscated too."

"What are you going to do with them?" Rich asked.

"Ciggies, fine. But you can't chuck away his phone. And he put his lighter inside the cigarette packet."

"Then I'll put them somewhere he won't find them," she said.

"He'll go ape," Rich said.

Jade grinned. "I know." She headed for the bedroom.

Rich stared at the empty space on the table where the cigarettes and phone had been. There was a new pack of cigarettes on a table in the hall, and he fetched it and put it on top of the TV. After a moment's thought, Rich tore the cellophane wrapper off the pack. Maybe Chance would assume he'd opened a new pack and not get too angry when he couldn't find his phone or his lighter.

Rich didn't ask where Jade was actually hiding Chance's stuff. He wasn't sure he wanted to know. And when Jade returned and moved on to the kitchen, he decided he really didn't want to know and went to the bedroom. He pushed the door shut and tried to read. He couldn't concentrate, and when he heard the study door open, he cringed.

A few moments later, he heard the explosion he had anticipated.

"What do you think you're doing?" Chance shouted.

Rich took a deep breath, then went to see what was happening.

Jade had been pouring beer down the kitchen sink. Empty bottles were neatly arranged on the counter, and now she'd started on the champagne. The room reeked of alcohol.

Jade and Chance were staring at each other, and Rich would not have put money on who would blink or look away first.

"Let's just all calm down," Rich said. His voice seemed quiet and strained and rather weedy, even to himself.

"I am calm," Jade said. She didn't sound it.

"Maybe we should"—Rich swallowed—"talk about this."

"I've nothing to say," Jade replied. She was still locked in a staring match with her father.

"Fine," Chance said. "Then you can listen. Both of you." He broke from the confrontation with Jade as he turned to glare at Rich. "In the living room. Now."

"I don't—" Jade started to say.

"Now!"

She didn't finish the thought. She pushed past Chance and Rich and went and sat on the sofa. Rich hesitated a moment, then went and sat beside her.

Chance stood in front of the fireplace, facing them. He looked down at the coffee table between them.

"Where are my cigarettes?"

"I don't know," Rich said. "Haven't seen them. On top of the TV, maybe?"

"So you're going to smoke at us again, are you?" Jade asked.

"I'm going to tell you some things that you may not want to hear," Chance said, surprisingly calm. "And some things that you may not believe, but need to know."

"So no slouching at the back," Jade muttered.

Despite himself, Rich giggled.

"Absolutely," Chance told them, deadly serious. "It's bad for your posture." His mouth twitched, just slightly. But it was enough to defuse the tension a little. He took a deep breath, as if gathering himself for what he was going to say.

Rich waited to be shouted at. He and Jade were used to being told off by their mum, and despite her bravado, Rich knew that Jade didn't like it. He could feel how tense she was. He just hoped she'd take it and not yell back like she sometimes did at Mum. Or used to.

But Chance didn't shout. When he spoke, his voice was calm and quiet. "You've been through a lot," he said. "I know it hasn't been easy for you, even without the upheaval of coming here and coping with me. It's difficult, losing someone you love. Especially the first time."

"Like you'd know," Jade said.

"I said you might not believe what I say," Chance told her. "But I do know. I lost both my parents before I was twenty. But this isn't about me, it's about you. Right now it's you two who are important. We don't know each other yet, let's not even pretend that we do, but I hope we will. I guess there's never a good time for what's happened, but right now may be even more awkward than it should be."

"Why?" Rich asked.

Chance sighed. "One of the most awkward things is that I can't tell you. Not at the moment. There are things about . . ." He hesitated, deciding how to phrase what he wanted to say. ". . . things about my job that I can't tell you right now."

"Like why you have a security thing on the phone?" Jade asked.

He nodded. "It's a scrambler. For secure conversations. My work is important and it's taking up a lot of my time just now. I have some things I need to finish up—urgent things. I can't have distractions."

"Is that what we are?" Jade said.

Chance smiled. "With the best will in the world, what do you think? I'd love for it to be possible for you to just move in here and settle down and all of us to carry on as if nothing's changed. But that isn't possible. Things have changed—changed radically, for you and for me. We need time to come to terms with that, and to make it work." He leaned forward and looked at them both intently. "And I do want it to work. I really do. I want to get this right, for all our sakes."

"Cruel to be kind?" Jade wondered.

"Nothing so calculated," Chance told her. "I just need time to sort things out."

"So you dump us at boarding school so you can get your work done."

Chance sighed again. "I suppose that's what it comes down to. I know you don't like the idea—I don't like the idea either—but I'm afraid that's how it has to be."

"But why?" Rich asked.

"I'll tell you why as soon as I can," he promised. "Really I will. You don't know me, but I'm asking you to trust me. This is the best way. Till the end of term—a few weeks. Then we'll discuss it properly." He nodded to Rich. "And I mean discuss it. And we'll decide together what to do next, what's best. As a family. Deal?"

Neither Jade nor Rich said anything.

"Like I said," Chance went on. "I don't expect you to like it. But I hope you'll trust me enough to take my word."

"That's not fair," Jade said.

"I'll tell you what's not fair," Chance said quietly. "I could have ignored the call from Mrs. Gilpin. I could have told her that I never even saw my children, or that I don't think they're mine at all, or that I'm just not interested in my own kids. They don't want to know me, so why should I want to know them, look after them? Put myself out for them? Change my entire life for them? Just because they lost their mum and there's no one else? But I didn't. Because that wouldn't be fair. It really wouldn't."

Both Rich and Jade were looking down at the floor. By the time they looked up again, Chance had gone.

"Maybe we should give him a break," Rich said to Jade. "Give him back his phone and cigarettes." Rich could sense Jade was tense. "You can't keep blaming him for what happened to Mum."

"Just because he suddenly goes all slushy and says he cares doesn't mean it's true," Jade protested.

"He said we'd talk," Rich pointed out.

"Yeah, after he's packed us off to school. Then what? A live-in nanny for the holidays so he can get on with this important job of his? So he can build his career without being distracted? Well, Mary Poppins we don't need."

"I'm going to tell him you took his cell phone and his ciggies," Rich decided. "And the lighter."

"You creep!" Jade tried to grab Rich, but he was already on his way to the study.

They heard the phone ring and both stopped, close to the study door.

The door was open a fraction and they could hear Chance's voice from inside.

"No, not at the flat," he was saying. "Too many . . . distractions right now."

"He means us," Jade mouthed at Rich.

"I know," he mouthed back. "We shouldn't be listening," he whispered. But neither of them moved away from the door.

"I have it safe," Chance was saying. "I'll bring it with me. Be happy to get it to someone who knows what to do with the stuff. I can't risk them finding it."

"Does he mean us again?" Jade murmured.

Rich shrugged.

"Half an hour then," Chance was saying. "Somewhere safe where we can talk and I can hand it over to you. Don't come here, though, whatever you do. . . . Because I'm telling you." He sounded angry now. "Put them in danger, and it'll be the last time I work for you. Ever." There was a pause. "That old scrap yard? Yes, I know it. Totters Lane, isn't it? Yes. Half an hour."

Jade grabbed Rich's arm and pulled him into the bedroom.

"What?" Rich said.

"What do you mean, 'what'? If this job of his is so important and if it's on the level, and if he really does work in the oil industry . . ."

"If?" Rich countered.

"Yes, if. If that's all true, then why is he going to a meeting to hand over something he shouldn't have, in a scrap yard?"

Rich sighed. "All right. Look, he said there were things he couldn't tell us right now. But maybe we should find out."

"Yeah? Like how?"

"By following him and seeing who he meets."

"We can't do that," Jade said. "Can we?"

Rich shrugged. "You can nick his cell phone—I don't see why we can't follow him to a meeting."

The bedroom door opened and Chance was standing there. "Look, sorry," he said. "I have to go out. We'll talk again when I get back, all right?"

"All right," Jade said.

They watched him cross the living room. He paused to pick up his cigarettes from on top of the television. He seemed about to open the pack, but he caught sight of Jade and Rich still watching him, and instead stuffed the cigarettes into his jacket pocket.

"See you in an hour or so then," Chance said. He didn't wait for a reply.

They heard the hall door slam shut behind him.

"We'll see you a lot sooner than that," Rich said.

7

The evening had drawn in and it was getting dark. There was a light drizzle, enough to permeate through Jade's coat and make the air feel colder than it was.

"There he is, look," Rich said, pointing to the dark silhouette of a figure passing under a streetlight farther down the road. They hurried after Chance, keeping to the shadows in case he looked back.

He did not look back, and Jade could not believe he knew they were following him. But then Chance suddenly darted into an alleyway. If she had blinked, Jade would have missed it—it would have seemed like he had simply disappeared into thin air.

They approached the end of the alley hesitantly, in case Chance was standing waiting for them. Jade wasn't frightened of him, but she didn't fancy another argument. For all her bravado, she didn't like falling out with anyone—even when they were wrong.

Rich looked at her, and Jade nodded. "Let's do it," she said quietly.

Together, they stepped into the end of the alley and looked around.

Nothing.

The alley was empty.

Chance was gone.

They sprinted along the alley and found it turned a sharp corner and then came out in a busy street. A bus sprayed water up at them as it went through a shallow puddle. People walked past quickly, huddled into their coats as the rain got heavier. Cars and taxis splashed after the bus.

There was no sign of John Chance.

"It's like he knew we were following him," Rich complained.

"How could he, though?" Jade said.

"Maybe he just thought someone might follow him," Rich said. "Not us, but someone else. I don't know. We need to find a bookstore."

Jade stared at him. "No—we need to find Dad."

"So he's 'Dad' now, is he?" Rich seemed amused.

"What else should I call him? And what good will a bookstore do? Or do you just want to get something to read?"

As they walked along the street, a woman with long black hair stepped out of the shadows. She was careful to keep well back, though neither of the twins had noticed she had been following them since they left the flat.

There was a bookstore farther down the same road. It was a small branch of a big chain, and it had what Rich wanted—an A to Z guide to London.

"Gonna look him up in the index?" Jade suggested. " 'John Chance is here' with a big arrow, maybe?"

In reply, Rich pointed to part of one of the maps. "That's where we are now, right? Just there."

"So?"

Rich moved his finger across to the facing page. "This is Totters Lane."

"Of course. Where the scrap yard is. How much is the book?"

Rich closed it and put it back on the shelf. "Dunno," he said. "But I can remember the way from the map. Come on, we've got fifteen minutes before his meeting."

The moment they were out of the store, the woman who had been standing on the other side of the bookcase, listening carefully, took a cell phone from her small handbag.

"Totters Lane," she said, as soon as the call was answered. "The scrap yard. He'll be there in about ten minutes."

· · ·

Chance paused to have a cigarette. He was surprised to find the packet was full.

He stared at the tightly packed ends of the cigarettes and frowned. He had not finished the previous pack, and his lighter had been inside. His mind raced through the possibilities. He checked his watch, and decided it was too late to get back to the flat and have it out with Jade and Rich. He had to be at the scrap yard in less than ten minutes. He'd decide what to do then.

In the meantime, he had a box of matches in his pocket. He could at least have a smoke.

Ten minutes later, out of breath, Rich and Jade arrived at the scrap yard. Huge, heavy metal double gates were standing slightly open at the end of the lane. Jade eased through first, followed by Rich.

There were no lights inside the yard. The high gates and walls kept out most of the light from the streets outside. They found themselves in a world of shadows and silhouettes. There was an open area immediately inside the gates, where trucks and cars could drive in. After that the place was a jungle of discarded debris. Cars were piled on top of each other, crushed down under the weight from above. Baby strollers and old shopping carts, iron bedsteads and old bicycles lay in heaps. Pages of old newspaper blew like tumbleweed through the landscape.

"This place is huge," Jade said. She spoke in a hushed whisper, as if the dead cars might hear her.

"He could be anywhere," Rich agreed.

As he finished speaking, there was a sound from behind them—a rasping, scraping sound as the heavy gates were being pushed open. Rich grabbed Jade's hand and they ran for the nearest shadows, hiding in the darkness by the gutted shell of an old Ford.

A dark shape pushed into the yard and stood in the darkness inside the gates. There was a flare of light as the figure struck a match, and the twins could see that it was their father. He lit a cigarette and flicked the match away.

"He took his time," Jade whispered.

"Came the long way," Rich whispered back. "Making sure he wasn't being followed, remember?"

"But who is he meeting?"

As Jade spoke, they could hear the sound of an engine—a vehicle approaching at high speed. Chance had heard it too, and he moved quickly away from the gates, obviously expecting them to be pushed open.

They exploded as a large blue van crashed through into the open area inside the yard. It screeched to a halt, skidding on the wet ground. Two men leaped out and ran straight at Chance. A heavy crowbar caught the light from the street outside the shattered gates as one of the men raised it over Chance's head.

Jade cried out, but no one apart from Rich heard.

The heavy bar crashed down. Chance stepped neatly

aside and slammed his elbow into the man's stomach. The attacker doubled over, dropping the bar. Chance immediately grabbed him tight around the neck and spun him around into the other attacker. Both assailants went down with a cry of pain.

Chance stepped back, ready for them to come at him again.

One of the men produced a gun from his waistband. There was the staccato crack of a shot followed by the sound of the bullet impacting in the ground close to Chance. Then a blur of movement as Chance was running—straight at the man with the gun. He kicked out and the gun went flying.

"We should help," Jade said. But she was frozen to the spot as she watched.

"Not sure he needs help," Rich said as Chance slammed his fist into the shooter's face. Both twins winced as they heard the crack of knuckles on jawbone.

But two more men had appeared from the back of the van and were rushing at Chance. The man who had lost the gun was groaning on the floor. The man with the crowbar had recovered enough to join his fellows as they dived on Chance.

Jade started across the yard, but Rich grabbed her arm. "No! There's nothing we can do," he said. "They've got guns—look."

The two newcomers had handguns leveled at Chance, who put his arms up in surrender. As soon as it was clear that he was not a threat anymore, one of the men stepped forward and thumped him over the head with his gun. Chance collapsed to his knees. He looked up at the man who had hit him, and Jade could see that her dad's face was full of anger, rather than fear or pain.

Then Chance's gaze shifted—looking past his attackers, straight at Jade, as she stood in full view, outside the protective shadows. He gave the slightest shake of his head, the slightest smile. Rich grabbed hold of Jade's hand and pulled her back into the darkness.

The men led Chance to the van and bundled him into the back. The doors slammed shut behind them, then the van turned in a slow circle and drove out through the broken gates.

Jade and Rich waited a moment, then walked slowly after the van, out into the street. Neither of them spoke. And neither of them noticed the woman with long black hair who stood in a dark doorway farther along the street. Nor did they see the man in a long gray raincoat standing in the shadows outside the gates. But the woman did. She watched as the man took off his dark-framed glasses and wiped the rain from them with a crisply ironed white handkerchief. Then he waited until the twins were out of earshot before using his cell phone.

"Phillips here, sir," he said, as soon as his call was answered. "I came to meet Chance as arranged, but I'm afraid there's a bit of a problem." He watched the two children turn out of the end of the lane into the main street beyond. "Make that a couple of problems," he said gravely.

8

Rich and Jade stood at the end of the lane and looked up and down the main street.

"They had guns," Jade said. "Those men—they had guns!"

"I saw," Rich told her.

"In London. Britain. People don't have guns here."

"Jade, calm down," Rich said. "This isn't helping. We have to find Dad, okay?"

"Okay." Jade took a deep breath. "Which way did the van go?" she asked.

Rich shook his head.

"God, you're useless," she groaned.

"Yeah," he agreed. "And I s'pose you saw where it went—got the number and everything."

"God, *I'm* useless too. Who were they?"

"I don't know."

"Where were they taking him?"

"I don't know."

"What do they want with him?"

"Look, I'm useless, right?" Rich told her. "I don't know."

Jade was pacing back and forth, looking each way along the road. "What do we do? And don't say 'I don't know'—think of something. Anything."

"Well . . . ," Rich said. "We could go back to the flat and hope he turns up. Maybe it was some prank, some mates of his from work . . ."

"They had guns!" Jade said. "They beat him up. They weren't mucking about."

"No," Rich said quietly. "Can't you stand still a minute?" He sat down on the wet sidewalk and Jade slumped down beside him. "Maybe back at the flat," he said. "Maybe there's some clue about who these people are and why they want him and where they've taken him. Or if they let him go, he'll come back to the flat. Or call. Whatever."

"Perhaps the guys who took him will call," Jade said, "and demand a ransom."

"We don't have any money," Rich pointed out. "Anyway, you probably wouldn't pay to get him back."

Jade didn't answer that. "We could go to the police."

"Probably should," Rich agreed.

"If they believe us."

"We saw it. It happened. He's gone. They'll have to believe us."

Jade had her phone out. "999 then."

Rich shook his head. "I'd rather talk to a real person. Make sure they do something." He looked Jade in the eye. "He's our dad. He's all we've got."

She sighed. Then she nodded. "We'll get him back," she said. "Whatever he's up to, whatever he's involved in, whatever it takes—we'll get him back."

The inside of the police station was smaller than Jade had expected. There was a little seating area where several bored people were waiting, and a high desk with a computer on it. Behind the desk, Jade could see another room, and several policemen and -women were busy at their own computers.

There was a policeman standing at the desk—a sergeant, from the three stripes on his uniformed arm. He stared at Jade and Rich as they came in, then went back to writing in a book.

"Our dad's been kidnapped," Jade told him.

The sergeant looked up. "Kidnapped?" he said.

Jade nodded.

"Course he has," the sergeant said. "And I'm the pope."

"No, really, he has," Rich said. "And you're not the pope. You're a policeman and you're supposed to help us."

The sergeant sighed. "Then I suppose you'd better tell me all about it."

He listened while Jade and Rich gave an account of the evening's events. Then he said, "You don't seem to know your dad very well."

"We only just met him," Jade said.

"You only just met your dad?"

"We lived with our mum," Rich said. "Only she died. Now we're with Dad."

"And he's been kidnapped, by armed thugs in a van."

The sergeant turned away for a moment, as if checking with someone out of sight in the next room. "From a scrap yard," he repeated as he turned back.

"Yes," Jade insisted.

"Have you heard of wasting police time?" the sergeant asked.

"Yes," Rich said quickly, before Jade could reply. "But that isn't what we're doing."

"You think we want to be here with you?" Jade asked. She gave a sarcastic laugh.

The sergeant seemed to consider this. "All right, let me take some particulars and we'll see what we can do."

"Great. At last," Jade said.

"Names first," the sergeant said. "Yours and your father's."

They told him, and the sergeant tapped away at his computer.

"That's John with an *h*, is it?" the sergeant asked. "And how is Chance spelled?"

Rich spelled it out. The sergeant tapped away for a bit longer, then shook his head. "Nope," he told them.

"What do you mean, 'nope'?" Jade demanded.

"I can check all the public records from here—electoral roll, phone book, council tax records. And I can check police data too, and everyone who pays an electricity or gas bill."

"So?" Rich asked.

"So, there's no one called John Chance."

"Maybe he's registered at a different address," Rich said. "He's not been there that long."

"That's right," Jade agreed, remembering the letters addressed to the previous tenant.

But the sergeant was shaking his head. "I don't just mean that address. I've checked the database for the whole of London. There's no John Chance listed. Not anywhere closer than Bedfordshire." He leaned forward across the desk, his face serious and his voice low. "Perhaps you'd like to go away and think about that," he said.

Jade was about to reply—to tell him what she thought of him and his computer and its database. But Rich grabbed her arm.

"You're right. I think we'd better go," he said.

Jade caught the tone in his voice. He was right, of course—there was no point in arguing and getting into more trouble. She turned and stamped out of the police station.

Rich and Jade walked back along the street, back in the direction of the flat.

Rich paused and looked back at the police station. "It's not like it's that unusual a name, is it? No one called John Chance? No one at all in the whole of London?"

"So, what are you saying?" Jade said.

"The policeman's lying. I don't know what's going on here, Jade. I don't know what we've got ourselves into. But I don't like it."

Back in the police station, the man who had been standing in the shadows of the doorway by the desk stepped forward and nodded to the desk sergeant.

"That was fine, thank you."

The sergeant said nothing. He didn't like deceiving anyone—especially children.

"They'll be all right," the man assured him. He regarded the sergeant through dark-framed glasses for a moment, then he buttoned his long gray raincoat and walked out of the door.

Andrew Phillips walked slowly along the street. Ahead of him he could see the Chance twins, heads down, heading back—he assumed—to their dad's flat. Not that it was really their dad's flat at all, of course. They'd find that out. They were clever kids. But that didn't make it any easier. Phillips sighed and pulled out his cell phone.

The small phone was slightly chunkier and heavier than it needed to be. The built-in scramblers were getting smaller, but they still bulked up the phone. Phillips pressed the key combination to activate the device that would encrypt his voice and decipher the scrambled voice data coming to him. Then he dialed a number.

The phone at the other end was answered at once.

"Mr. Ardman," Phillips said. "Just reporting progress." He gave a brief summary of events at the police station.

"You're not happy about this, are you, Andrew?" Ardman said when he had finished. "I can tell. I'm not happy either."

"They're just kids. They've already lost their mother."

"And now it seems that Vishinsky has their father. I agree, it doesn't look too good, does it?"

"That's the understatement of the year," Phillips muttered. The scrambler software in the phone amplified his words before encrypting them, so that Ardman would hear him.

Ardman's sigh of frustration was also amplified and relayed clearly. "If Vishinsky has Chance," the man said, "and I don't know who else could be behind this, then he's probably dead already. If not, he will be very soon. Which leaves only one question."

"What did Chance do with the sample? He hadn't had

a chance yet to get it to me safely, what with this business with the kids and the fact he was probably being watched by Vishinsky's people. So he must have hidden it."

"And we need to find it. Before Vishinsky does. Things don't look good, Andrew, I have to admit that. But there is the possibility that Chance is still alive and will hold out. There is also the possibility that his children know where the sample is hidden. If not, they may draw out Vishinsky's people, make them overplay their hand and reveal themselves. Either way it's worth keeping them in play. They may even be able to help us get their father back."

Phillips was not convinced. "Like you said, Chance's probably dead. But if he isn't . . ." His voice trailed off.

"Yes?" Ardman prompted.

"If he isn't," Phillips said, "and he finds out we've deliberately put his children in danger, then I for one won't be worrying about Vishinsky anymore. Will you?"

There was a pause at the other end of the phone as Ardman considered this. "Probably not," he agreed at last. "In that scenario, I expect we're all dead."

John Chance opened his eyes, but he already knew he would see nothing—he could feel the hood over his head. From the low humming sound and the slight feeling of motion, he could tell he was on a plane—a small plane, probably a private jet. He could guess who it belonged to. He shifted position very slightly, just enough to establish that his wrists and ankles were tied. Just enough to be sure there were no easy means of escape.

No, he'd have to sit this out. For the moment. Vishinsky would want to know where the sample of fluid was hidden. Chance knew that as long as he didn't reveal its whereabouts, he had a chance of staying alive. The irony, of course, was that he didn't actually know where the sample was.

He closed his eyes, not that it made much difference, and prepared for a long and boring journey. Best to conserve his strength for any chance, however slight, of escape. He wasn't bitter. He didn't blame anyone for his current predicament—it was an occupational hazard. But he was annoyed that he hadn't managed to pack Rich and Jade off to school yet. He was irritated and concerned that they had seen what happened at the scrap yard. And he was determined that whatever fate awaited him, nothing would harm his children . . .

9

When the hood came off, John Chance was left blinking in the sudden light. The first thing he saw was
the curved ceiling of the plane. He was in a large comfortable seat. There was no row in front, just an open
space until the bulkhead a long way in front—comfort
and style, Chance thought. Except, of course, that he was
tied up.

"Boris Yeltsin himself sat in that seat," a voice said. It
was rich and deep, speaking English with a heavy Russian
accent. "Several times."

"Fancy that." Chance's reply was barely more than a croak. "Doesn't seem like there's enough room."

"Our guest is thirsty," the voice said. "Probably tired as well. Traveling is such hard work."

The man with the rich voice appeared in front of Chance. He was a tall man, slightly stooped, with hair that was so gray it was almost white. He was dressed immaculately in an expensive handmade gray suit.

"Viktor Vishinsky," the tall gray-haired man said. "I'm delighted you could join me."

"How could I refuse?" Chance's voice was stronger now. He held out his hands—tied together at the wrist. His ankles were tied as well, and he could feel the cords biting into his flesh. Straps held him tight in the chair. "You'll forgive me if I don't shake your hand, but . . ." He let the words hang.

"But you are rather tied up at the moment," Vishinsky said. Teeth appeared in his thin face, but there was no other indication that he was amused. His eyes remained cruel and gray.

". . . I never shake hands with insects like you," Chance went on as if the man had not spoken.

There was a moment's pause. Then what there was of the smile vanished. At the same time, a fist slammed into Chance's stomach. He wanted to double up with the pain, but could not move because of the straps holding him to the chair. A large man in a white steward's uniform smiled at Chance's pain and flexed his hand.

"Please, please," Vishinsky admonished. He sounded reasonable and calm and friendly. But Chance knew the man would kill him without hesitation when it suited him.

Vishinsky was speaking again. "I know who you are, Mr. Lessiter," he said. Chance smiled at the use of his alias. The smile faded as Vishinsky went on: "Or should I say, Mr. Chance."

"You brought me all this way to check my résumé, did you?" Chance said.

"No. But I must apologize," Vishinsky was saying, "for not realizing sooner that I had such a talented gentleman on my staff. I shall have to make sure that KOS checks up on the so-called experts it employs rather more diligently in the future."

"Always best to check references," Chance said quietly.

Vishinsky ignored him. "But in the meantime, what are we to do with you?" he wondered, leaning forward to stare into Chance's face. "Kill you?"

"Your people could have done that in London," Chance pointed out. "You didn't need to put me on a plane first."

"And where do you think we might be going?" Vishinsky asked. He didn't wait for Chance's answer, but walked slowly over to a table fixed to the floor on the other side of the wide cabin. He helped himself to a drink from a decanter—colorless liquid that Chance guessed was vodka.

"I imagine we're heading for Krejikistan," Chance said.

"Either to the headquarters of Krejikistan Oil Subsidiaries or to your own humble abode."

"Oh, I have several humble abodes." Vishinsky sipped at the vodka. "Do go on, this is most illuminating."

"Very well. I imagine you've gone to all the trouble of kidnapping me because you want something from me. Something more than amusing conversation."

"You know what I want," Vishinsky said.

"Do I?"

"Oh, I think you do." Vishinsky seemed amused rather than angry. "And I expect you're wondering what it is and why we need it. That small sample of fluid you took from my London installation."

Chance could not help but smile. "I expect you want it because we blew the rest of it up, so that sample—assuming I even took a sample—would be all that's left."

"We know you took a sample," Stabb said. "We have the CCTV footage. We saw you at the canister."

"You think," Chance said. "But whether I took a sample or not, why don't you just make more of the stuff?"

Vishinsky glanced at the steward, who looked like he was about to thump Chance again, but after a moment Vishinsky held up his hand to stop the attack.

"It is a very complicated formula which was unfortunately known only to the scientist who created it. Of course, it would be easy enough to reverse engineer that formula, given a sample of the fluid. And you have a sample."

"But you," Chance said, "have the scientist and his

research . . ." Then he laughed as he realized. "No, you don't, do you. What happened? Did you get rid of him too soon? Assume he'd documented his research when he hadn't bothered, or hidden it too well?"

"There was an accident." Vishinsky sounded angry now. He drained his glass and refilled it. "The man's car . . . It was very unfortunate."

"I bet."

"But for your information, he detailed his research meticulously. We made sure of that first. You think we are stupid? But his notes, his paperwork . . ." He stopped, his eyes narrowing.

"Don't tell me you can't find it," Chance said. "Don't tell me the poor man hid it as insurance. In the vain hope you wouldn't actually kill him so he couldn't reproduce his work for anyone else."

"He didn't hide it," Vishinsky said. "It is, as I said, unfortunate. But he kept his notes and papers with him at all times."

"Took it to the grave, did he?"

"The car was just supposed to crash," Vishinsky said. "But it caught fire."

"Oh." Chance did his best to sound mortified. "Oh, how terribly sad."

"It is sad, yes," Vishinsky agreed. "Because it means that we need you. Or rather, the sample you took. And it is especially sad that my friend Mr. Stabb will go to any lengths, inflict any pain, to make you tell us where it is hidden."

"Even so, why should I? What's in it for me?"

"For you?" Vishinsky was smiling again. "An easy, quick, painless death."

"And for you?"

"Let's just say it would increase my standing considerably."

"Because of this formula, this fluid sample you think I have?" Chance asked.

"Exactly so," Vishinsky said, raising his glass as if in a toast.

Chance laughed.

"Tell me where it is," Vishinsky demanded.

"You might find this hard to believe, but I actually don't know."

The steward moved quickly. Another punch. Even harder. But Chance had been expecting it and managed to tense his stomach muscles so it didn't feel quite so bad.

"Do you know a man called Andrew Phillips?" Vishinsky asked.

"Never heard of him," Chance lied.

"We have photos of you meeting him several times while you were working at KOS. In some very strange places. Even at the scrap yard where we picked you up last night. Would you believe it, but he was there too? One of my associates happened to see him leaving and followed. I expect Mr. Stabb will know exactly where he is now."

"Really." Chance tried to sound bored.

Vishinsky nodded. "Really. And I think perhaps we'll ask Mr. Phillips where this fluid sample might be. If he knows, then I'm afraid we won't be needing your services anymore."

"Tragic."

"For you, yes. But if he doesn't know, I shall be wanting to talk to you again."

"I'll look forward to that," Chance said.

"Mr. Stabb will stay in London to supervise matters there," Vishinsky said. "My people in London can talk to your friend Phillips as soon as is convenient. But if we get no satisfaction, then there are a couple of other young people they may need to talk to." He looked closely at Chance as if studying him for any change of expression, any hint of feeling. "But let's hope it doesn't have to come to that. I do so hate to see children suffer. Don't you?"

Chance met the man's gaze without blinking. His own face was a blank mask. "Their suffering will be nothing compared to yours."

10

"We could call Mrs. Gilpin," Jade said.

"And tell her what? That Dad's been kidnapped? That just sounds daft." Rich had slumped on the sofa, while Jade was pacing up and down in front of him. He had no idea what to do now, and Jade's constant movement was irritating him. But there was no point in arguing.

"I don't care how it sounds!" Jade told him. "It happened!"

Rich grunted. "I know. I was there, remember? Might as well call Charmaine. She'd be as much help."

"At least she'd believe us," Jade said. She flopped down beside her brother on the sofa. "What are we going to do?"

"We're going to find him," Rich said. "I don't know how, but we can't just sit around here while Dad's missing."

"Do you think . . ." Jade turned and looked away from him. "Do you think they'll . . ." She broke off, biting her lip.

"Kill him? I dunno. I really don't." Rich patted her gently on the shoulder. They needed to do something, he thought. Anything to feel busy and stop them getting too depressed. If Jade got in one of her moods, then she'd hide in her room and do nothing at all, which wouldn't help anyone. "Let's check Dad's stuff for clues."

"What clues?" Jade asked, following Rich through to the study.

"Don't know till we find them," he admitted. "But he was taken for a reason. If we can find out why, then we're a good way to knowing who. And then we work on where. Right?"

"Right." Jade wiped the back of her hand across her eyes and went over to the desk. She started leafing through the papers on it. "I guess we need addresses, phone numbers, anything."

"Do you think he was expecting to meet the men who took him?" Rich wondered. "He was certainly meeting someone."

"And if it wasn't them, who was it?" Jade agreed.

At that moment, a bell rang. It took a moment for either of them to realize that it was the doorbell—they hadn't heard it ring before. Then they were both running to see who was there.

As they reached the door, there was the sound of a key scraping into the lock.

"Dad?!" Rich exclaimed, throwing open the door.

The man standing outside, holding the key, was a stranger. He wore thick-rimmed glasses and a long rain-coat. His free hand was clutched to his chest inside the coat. He was swaying on his feet.

"Who the hell are you?" Jade demanded.

In answer, the man fell forward, and Rich was only just able to catch him and hold him up. "Help me get him in-side," he said.

"Why?" Jade wanted to know. "Who is he?"

"I don't know." Rich was gasping under the man's weight. "Just help, will you?"

The man seemed to have recovered enough to take some of his own weight. With the help of Rich and Jade he staggered through into the living room, where he collapsed on the sofa.

"Chance," he said, his voice rasping with the effort.

"He's not here," Rich said.

"Do you know where he is?" Jade demanded.

The man shook his head. "Is it safe? The sample—is it safe?"

"What sample? What's he talking about?" Jade leaned

over the man, staring him in the face. "Just who are you? Do you know what's happened to our dad?"

Even from where he was standing, Rich could see the man's eyes were glassy and unfocused. Rich rubbed his fingers and brought the man's hand up to his face. It was covered in blood. Not just a smear or a splash. It was like he was wearing a crimson glove. On the floor, Rich could see the red trail, leading across the room to the sofa.

Jade seemed to have realized there was something terribly wrong too. She stood upright slowly, as if hardly daring to move. She could see that the man's coat had flapped open. The man still had his hand to his chest and blood was seeping through his fingers, staining the whole of the front of his shirt.

"Oh, my God," Jade said quietly. "What's happened to you?"

"He's been shot," Rich realized with horror.

The man was struggling to speak. "Don't worry about me. Just . . . the sample."

Jade looked at Rich and then back at the man. "We don't know about any sample. We have no idea what you're talking about. Who *are* you?" she asked again.

"Phillips," the man gasped. Speaking seemed to be even more of a struggle now. "Andrew Phillips. Friend of Chance—your father."

Rich was watching as if through a fog. But it was clearing slowly. "I'll call an ambulance," he said. "The police."

Phillips shook his head. "Too late," he rasped. "Far too

late. Just get out. Make sure the sample is safe and get out before . . ." His words were smothered by a fit of coughing. A red trickle ran from the corner of his mouth.

"Don't be stupid," Jade told him. "We can't just leave you."

"Get out!" the man said again, more forcefully. He tried to heave himself up, but the effort was too much and he collapsed back on to the sofa. He reached inside his coat with his other hand, and when it came out again he was holding a gun—a flat, black pistol. "I'll do what I can for you," he said.

Rich stared at the gun. "Maybe we should do as he says." But he didn't think the man was threatening them. He was warning them about something—someone else. "You've lost a lot of blood," he said.

The man coughed and Rich realized he was trying to laugh. "Just a bit. Go on, get out of here. While you still can."

It was then that the window exploded. Glass showered across the carpet, followed by the wooden support struts as a large dark figure crashed into the room. Rich just had time to see that he was holding a handgun. It was pointing straight at him and Jade.

There was the crack of a shot. Rich flinched. But it was the man on the sofa—Phillips—who was shooting. Two shots in rapid succession.

The man from the window staggered back. His own gun went off, firing a single bullet into the ceiling. Then a third shot from Phillips cannoned into the man's chest and he was thrown backward—back out of the window.

If the man cried out, his voice was lost in the sound of the front door shattering. Rich ran to the window, sneakers crunching on broken glass and splinters of wood.

"We can't jump!" Jade yelled at him and he realized she was right. There was a rope hanging outside—how the man had gotten in. But it ended at the level of the window. He'd come down from the roof.

Jade grabbed Rich's hand and pulled him away, back toward the door from the hall.

"We can't go out there," Rich hissed at her. Already he could hear the thump of running feet. But Jade pulled him into cover behind the door. Just as two black-clad figures arrived in the opening.

Phillips had managed to twist around on the sofa. Rich could see the man, teeth gritted with pain, as he brought his gun to bear, shooting over the top of the sofa's back.

One of the figures in the doorway seemed to stumble. The other was holding a larger gun—like a rifle, but with a stocky barrel. A machine pistol. The noise it made was deafening, echoing around the room.

The force of the gunfire moved the sofa across the floor. Phillips had disappeared from sight. Ragged holes appeared in the plaster on the wall on the other side of the sofa, and Rich shuddered to think what was happening to Phillips himself. Then the bullets raked across the wall, cracking into the television, which exploded.

The man with the machine pistol had run into the room as he fired. The other man stumbled after him and dropped to the floor, aiming a handgun. Rich could see his black jersey was wet on one side, and guessed it was blood from where Phillips's shot had hit him.

But he didn't wait to see any more. He pulled Jade with him out of the unguarded door, desperate to be out of the room before either of the men turned and saw them.

He was almost quick enough. Almost, but not quite.

The man on the floor was reaching back to examine where he'd been shot, and caught sight of Rich and Jade out of the corner of his eye. He cried out and raised the pistol.

A bullet ripped into the wall of the hall as Rich and Jade ran for the front door. A second later, a deafening burst of automatic fire stitched a line of holes after them.

The front door was a shattered mess of wood. The hinges were twisted and broken. Rich and Jade pushed through, and Rich felt the sharp wood catch on his trousers. He didn't slow down.

"The elevator!" he yelled at Jade.

"Too slow," she yelled back. "Stairs."

She was right—the elevator wasn't there, and they didn't have time to wait for it. Dust and splinters were kicking up at Rich's feet, and he realized with shock that bullets were smacking into the floorboards. Rich hurled himself down the stairs, holding tight to Jade's hand.

The sound of the shooting seemed to have stopped, but

they kept running. Maybe the gunmen didn't dare chase them out into the street, didn't want to attract attention. But Rich wasn't about to take that for granted.

They didn't stop running until they were three streets away. Then they collapsed, gasping and panting, hands on knees, as they doubled over to get their breath back and make sense of what happened.

Carl, the man who had been shot by Phillips, was holding a towel from Chance's kitchen tight to his wound. It was folded over several times to form a pad. He was lucky the bullet had gone through the fleshy part of his abdomen, but it was bleeding a lot. With his other hand he was pulling everything out of each of the kitchen drawers in turn.

The other man, Ivan, was in the study. The computer was on the floor, the screen broken. Papers and books lay all over the place. The contents of the desk had been tipped onto the floor and the box on the phone line had been ripped off and thrown aside.

He moved on to the next room—a bedroom with two single beds in it. He pulled open a drawer, and found it was full of socks and underwear. There was a pack of cigarettes hidden in among the panties, together with a cell phone. The man gave a snort of laughter. Naughty girl.

"I don't think it's here," Carl yelled in Russian. He winced with the pain of shouting.

Ivan returned from the bedroom. "We have to check," he replied. "But quickly."

"No cooking oil even. Nothing that could be what we're looking for."

Ivan checked the fridge. "Milk?" He lifted out the carton. It was translucent plastic and he unscrewed the top to make sure. "Just milk."

"What about Alexei?"

Ivan sniffed. "Probably dead. But we should remove the body. Leave no trace. I hope you haven't bled on the carpet."

Carl paled at the thought. "They will find my DNA. They can trace me."

"Only if they have you on file," Ivan assured him. "And we don't exist. Anyway, by this time tomorrow we'll have you home. They won't find you there."

"And we won't find the sample here."

Ivan sighed. "I think you're right. If anyone knows where to find it, my money is on those kids."

"Do we go after them?"

Carl shook his head. "Not us. At least, not yet. But if we do find them . . ." He did not need to complete the thought. He smiled.

The woman had been standing on the street opposite the house when Rich and Jade ran out. Her long black hair caught in the breeze, blowing around her as she walked quickly but without apparent haste after the two running figures.

She stopped in the shadows a hundred yards from where

the twins were, gasping for breath, watching them carefully, wondering how best to approach them and win their confidence. It was vitally important that they trust her and believe what she had to tell them. She had to make them understand that she was the only person in the world who could help them now . . .

11

Stabb waited for Ivan and Carl at his hotel. He was staying at the Gloucester, one of the larger, better hotels in Central London. After supervising the capture of Chance and seeing him safely onto the plane, Stabb had spent a few minutes updating Vishinsky. He was surprised his employer had come in person to collect Chance. Surprised and a little unsettled. It seemed from subsequent videophone conversations that Chance was not being cooperative.

So perhaps, Stabb thought, he should have gone with Ivan, Alexei and Carl to find Phillips.

This thought was reinforced by the phone call he took on his cell in the hotel's concierge lounge. It was nearly five in the morning and the lounge was almost deserted. Certainly, there was no one within earshot.

"Killing Phillips was not the plan," Stabb said, keeping his voice quiet. "We needed to find the sample. If Phillips is dead, he can tell us nothing. I thought we made it very simple for you."

"You told us where he was, not that he was armed," Ivan protested from the other end of the phone. "He went to Chance's flat, so we assumed he was collecting the sample."

"You assumed! You should have checked, made certain."

"We got into a shoot-out. We had no choice." There was a pause before Ivan added nervously, "Alexei is dead. And Carl took a bullet too. It isn't bad but he's very weak. It won't stop bleeding. I can't take him to a hospital."

"No, you can't," Stabb said quickly. This was becoming a nightmare. "So where was Phillips when you killed him? Where is he now?"

"In Chance's flat."

"Which is probably crawling with police by now."

"I doubt it. The shots were muffled and it's a pretty solid building. The floors above and below Chance are empty. Deaf woman on the ground floor. Not sure about the top. Students, I think. Probably slept right through it."

"But you didn't wait to find out," Stabb guessed.

Ivan sounded hurt. "We searched the place, top to bottom."

"And what did you find?"

"Nothing. Nothing at all. The sample isn't there."

Stabb sighed. "This is a mess. Now we have no leads at all."

"Except the kids."

"What? The kids were there? Tell me the kids weren't there, Ivan!"

"They got away, but—"

"But nothing. We'd better meet. But not here. I don't want Carl bleeding on the hotel carpet. By the west entrance to the underground garage where we met before. In ten minutes." He ended the call and tapped the small phone against his palm as he considered what to do.

Exactly ten minutes later, Ivan was explaining in more detail what had happened. Stabb listened without comment. They were standing inside the underground garage—a forest of concrete pillars supporting the building above. Carl was leaning against the side of a car, breathing heavily. There was a sheen of sweat across his face and he was clutching at his side. Stabb could see where the blood was leaking through his clothes.

"All right," Stabb said when they were done. "There's nothing more we can do for the moment. It's out of our hands for now. But be ready, Ivan—I may need you again soon."

Ivan said, "What about Carl?"

"Ivan said you can get me out of the country," Carl said. His voice was throaty and hoarse. "Make me disappear."

Stabb nodded. "We can't afford any loose ends—that's for sure." He held out a gloved hand toward Carl. "Give me your gun."

Carl struggled to pull the handgun from his jacket and handed it to Stabb.

"Yes," Stabb said, turning the gun over and examining it. He chambered a round. "I can make you disappear." Then he leveled the gun and shot Carl through the forehead.

"Get rid of him," Stabb told Ivan, handing him the gun. "It's easier to get rid of a body than a wounded man."

Ivan looked down at the corpse slumped against a wheel of the car. "I shall bear that in mind," he said.

The Internet café didn't open till nine and it was barely six, so Rich and Jade found a place that was open for early breakfast. It was smoky and greasy and the ketchup on the tables was in red tomato-shaped plastic bottles that had crusted nozzles.

But the man serving the first customers of the day was friendly enough. Jade guessed from the size of him that he ate what he served—all of which seemed to be fried.

"Don't suppose you have a vegetarian option?" she asked.

The man just stared at her.

"Like juice and some fruit or cereal?" Jade tried.

The man stared some more. Then he slowly shook his head.

"Okay," she said. "Toast. Surely you can do toast?"

"I'll have a bacon sandwich," Rich said. "And coffee."

"Tea," Jade said.

"One bacon sarney, a tea and a coffee," the man said. "And some toast."

They sat where they had a good view of the street. Not that Jade expected the men from the flat to find them, but she kept a nervous watch. The street was getting busy as morning arrived and London came to life. It was amazing how early some people were up and off to work.

They ate in silence.

When they were finished, Rich said, "You think we should go back to the flat?"

His voice was hushed and nervous as he remembered what had happened there.

"And what if those men are still waiting for us—we could have been killed!" Jade looked around, as if expecting them to come into the café, guns ready. "We could call the police."

"They were no help before," Rich said. "And most police in this country aren't armed. What can we do?"

"There's a body now," Jade whispered. She hated thinking about it, but there was no avoiding how real the body was. "That would convince them, surely."

"If it's still there."

A shadow fell across the table. Jade looked up, assuming it was the man from the counter. Instead it was a woman holding a mug of tea.

"Do you mind if I join you?" the woman asked.

"There's lots of other tables," Jade pointed out. "And we're having a private conversation actually," she added quickly.

But the woman sat down anyway, despite Jade's words and her glare.

"I know," she said, her voice accented with a foreign lilt. "About your father, I expect. And what happened at the flat."

Jade and Rich stared at her. She was strikingly attractive, with narrow features and black hair that hung down almost to her waist. Her jacket looked like it came from a top fashion shop. She smiled at them.

"Look, who are you?" Jade demanded.

"My name is Magda Kornilov. I am a colleague of your father's," the woman said. "I want to help him. To help you. If you will let me."

Jade looked at Rich. He shrugged. "How can you help us?" Jade asked.

"I can tell you what he was doing and why he was taken."

"Then you know . . . ," Rich started. He broke off as if unsure how much to say.

Magda nodded. "I know everything. I know your father worked for an oil company called KOS. I know he didn't want you two around just at the moment because he was worried you would find out what he is really up to."

"And what's that?" Jade wanted to know.

"He is a spy," Magda said. She sipped at her tea. "This is very good."

"A spy?" Jade asked, incredulous.

"An industrial spy, not like James Bond." Magda put down her mug and mimed shooting Jade with her fingers. "Bang, bang." Her smile faded. "Though there is a lot of that, I am afraid, especially when you play for such high stakes."

"Tell us," Rich said. "We're listening."

"Very well. At the oil company, at KOS, they know your father as Mr. Lessiter, an expert in oil refining and polymer chemistry. There is a real Mr. Lessiter, of course, and that is who they thought they had employed."

"Those letters—the ones Dad threw away," Rich said to Jade. "Remember? They were addressed to someone called Lessiter."

"Your father is living in Lessiter's flat," Magda said. "Lessiter is away—paid off, or hidden, or perhaps even held captive." She shrugged. "I don't know which."

"Why should we believe you?" Jade asked.

"It's up to you. I'm asking for nothing. I'm offering to help. Believe me or not, but I am telling you why your father was not in his own flat, did not get his own mail, did not want you around, encrypted his phone conversations. And was kidnapped."

"Because he's an industrial spy," Rich said.

Magda nodded. "KOS has developed a new formula—when added to petrol and other fuel oils it makes them far more efficient. You can run a car for longer on a liter of treated petrol. Airliners can travel farther without refueling. You can imagine how valuable such a formula would be. Your father stole it."

"Never!" Jade exclaimed. There was a lull in the background noise as people in the café turned to look. "I don't believe you," Jade said more quietly. Rich shifted in embarrassment.

Magda smiled and sipped her tea. "It explains away many things that have worried you. Why not believe it?"

"Are you saying that these KOS people—the oil company—that they found out?" Rich asked. "Found out and took him? Why would they do that?"

"They would not," Magda said. "I work for KOS. I know. It was not them, though your father did steal a sample of treated fuel which we very much want back."

"Then who took him?" Jade demanded. She was leaning back with her arms folded.

"KOS does a lot of work for the Ministry of Defense. Sensitive work. Anyone spying on KOS might have access to sensitive material that could harm British defense. There are security considerations." Magda leaned across the table toward them. "Did you wonder why the police were so unwilling to help? Why they did nothing—even when there is a shoot-out in the middle of London they do nothing?"

Rich and Jade exchanged looks. "Go on," Rich said.

"Because your father was not kidnapped. He was arrested, though he will never come to trial. I imagine he no longer officially even exists."

Jade shivered as she remembered their visit to the police station, the fact there was apparently no record of their father. "But who took him?"

"The security services. MI5 or MI6, it doesn't matter which."

Rich frowned. "Why are you telling us this?"

"I worked with your father at KOS. Okay, he is a spy, but I liked him. I think the security services have overreacted." She lowered her voice. "They killed Phillips," she said. "He was your father's contact. Another spy. And they shot him down."

"He had a gun," Rich pointed out.

Jade frowned at him.

"They were shooting at him," Rich went on. "He was wounded, remember. They shot at us, Jade." He turned to Magda. "Thank you for telling us this."

"What's in it for you?" Jade asked.

"I just want to help. It's a tough business, and children should not be involved."

"And that's it?" Jade said.

"That's it. Although if I could find the sample of fuel

that your father took, that would be of immense help. Its return would give us something to bargain with. Something I could take to KOS and tell them to ask MI5 for your father's release." She sipped her tea. "Do you know where he hid it?"

"You just want this fuel sample back," Jade said.

Magda nodded. "And if we can return what was stolen, then everything will be fine."

"Will it?" Jade wondered.

"It couldn't hurt," Rich said. "Only, we have no idea where it is."

Magda's expression didn't change. "He never mentioned it? You didn't see him hide something?"

They both shook their heads.

"Maybe he gave you something to look after for him?" Magda suggested. "Told you it was important and not to say anything to anyone about it."

"Nothing like that," Rich told her. "We only met him a couple of days ago."

"Ah yes," Magda said. "Your mother's death. I am sorry."

Jade looked away. Rich took her hand, holding it below the level of the table, so that the woman would not see. Jade took a deep breath and turned back to face the woman. "I think you should go now," she told her.

"I am sorry," Magda said again. "But if you think of anything, anything at all, call me." She handed Rich a slip of paper with a phone number on it. "That is my cell number. I want to help you, but . . ." She shrugged. "No pressure, okay?"

Jade nodded. "Okay."

Rich turned back to face Magda. "Thank you," he said.

Magda met his gaze. "I lost my mother too, when I was young. Perhaps no older than you. I know how it feels—how you must feel. I really am very sorry. I really do want to help."

"Thanks," Rich said quietly.

Jade said nothing, but tears were welling up in her eyes.

Magda nodded, smiled and walked out of the café. She did not look back.

"You believe her?" Jade asked as soon as the woman was gone. She wiped her sleeve across her eyes.

"I think so," Rich said. "Why would she lie?"

"Are you kidding? She wants this fuel sample stuff."

"At least she isn't shooting at us. Like she said—no pressure."

"I suppose," Jade conceded.

"And if we find it, or work out where it is, then this sample—it might get Dad back."

"*If* we want him back," Jade said quietly. "An industrial spy—what sort of dad is that?"

"We won't know if we don't find him," Rich pointed out. "Keep her cell number just in case."

Jade frowned as a thought occurred to her. "Hang on . . ."

"What?"

"Dad's cell phone."

"You think we can call him up and ask him where he is?"

"Don't be daft. He hasn't got it. I hid it. With his cigarettes, remember?"

"Oh, yeah. So?"

"So it'll have contact numbers in it. People we can talk to—get help from."

"Maybe," Rich said. "Let's see."

Jade sighed. "I haven't got it with me."

"Back at the flat?" Rich sighed. "Terrific. That's one place we don't want to go back to."

Jade nodded. "But it's the last place they'll expect us. If those men have gone . . ."

"We could check it out, I suppose," Rich said cautiously. "Just take a look. And then if the coast is clear there's other stuff we might need too."

"You mean like a change of clothes."

"I mean like money. And passports." He nodded slowly as he thought about it. "Might be worth the risk. Just about."

"There's a dead guy on the floor," Jade said quietly.

"I know." Rich met her gaze. "You all right?"

Jade shrugged. "Guess we'll have to find out."

12

The lock on the front door to the building was broken. Rich hadn't noticed in their haste to leave. But the place seemed quiet, so maybe no one else had either. Rich couldn't remember seeing anyone else in the building at all. Perhaps Dad had the only occupied flat.

The bullet holes spattered across the wall close to the top of the stairs gave them pause for thought.

"You sure about this?" Rich asked apprehensively.

"No," Jade told him. "But what else can we do?"

"Go to the police. They can't deny the bullet holes exist."

"And if Magda is right and they're in on it? Maybe we'd disappear too."

Rich couldn't think of an answer to that. So he followed Jade as she tiptoed to the shattered remains of the door to the flat and waited at the door. Together, they listened for the slightest sound. But there was nothing. Just cars from the street outside. Somewhere, a dog barked.

"Come on then," Rich said. He just wanted to get it over with. He found that hanging around not knowing what was happening was the worst thing.

Inside the flat, the picture of the train was on the floor, glass smashed and picture torn. The upholstery had been ripped off the sofa. The curtains had been pulled down from over the shattered window—glass and wood strewn across the floor, together with books and papers and magazines. The television was a wreck. And there was a dead body lying facedown in the middle of the room.

Jade caught her breath as she saw it. She kept close to the walls, as far from the body as she could, making a point of not looking at it as she made her way around the room to the far door.

Rich also tried not to look at Phillips's body as he followed Jade quickly through to the bedroom. He glanced into the kitchen—and saw that too was a total mess, with everything emptied out over the floor and work surfaces.

The study door was open and Rich could see it was in

an even worse state than the other rooms. Only their bedroom didn't seem too bad, but even so, the pillows and mattresses had been cut open and the stuffing pulled out.

"Pretty thorough," Rich said.

"It's . . . awful," Jade said, looking around.

"You think they found Dad's cell phone?" Rich asked.

Jade went over to her bedside cabinet. The drawers were half-open and stuff had been pulled out. She pulled the top drawer completely open. "I hid it in here," she said.

Rich was amused, for what felt like the first time in ages. "In your underwear drawer."

"Didn't think he'd look there. Those men didn't anyway—not properly." She pulled out the phone and the pack of cigarettes.

"Bring those too," Rich said.

"Why?"

"Because he'll need a smoke if we ever find him."

Jade glared at him, but said nothing. She grabbed a small backpack from the mess on the floor and tipped it upside down. A book and some makeup fell out. She stuffed the phone and the cigarettes inside. "There are only a few cigarettes left," she said. "But his lighter is inside—he might want that back." She pushed clothes into the backpack.

Rich found his passport and tossed it over to her. "Stick that in too. I'll see if I can find any cash. Maybe a credit card—you never know."

"You can't use Dad's credit card!"

"He won't mind. We're on expenses. Wonder whose

name it'll be in—his or Lessiter's." His smile froze as he heard a sound.

Jade had heard it too. Something moving. Footsteps in the other room. Rich put his finger to his lips and walked slowly and quietly toward the door.

There was someone in the living room. A dark figure knelt beside the body on the floor. Rich crept as quietly as he could to the door, hoping to get a good look at the man and then duck out of sight without being spotted.

The man looked up—straight at Rich. "Hello, young man," he said. "I'd suggest a cup of tea, but I'm afraid the kitchen is a bit of a mess." He pulled a crisp white handkerchief out of his pocket.

Jade joined Rich in the doorway, backpack looped over her shoulder. The man stood up and regarded them both with interest. He was a tall, lean man, with short dark hair that was beginning to grow thin, and he wore a dark blue suit. His hand was stained with blood where he had examined Phillips's body, and he wiped it carefully on the handkerchief as he spoke.

"It probably sounds a bit inadequate," the man said, "but I do apologize for the inconvenience."

"Inconvenience?" Jade said. "He's dead!"

The man nodded. "It wasn't him to whom I was apologizing, actually." He smiled, but there was no humor in it. "Bit late to apologize to poor Phillips."

"You knew him?" Rich asked. "Do you work for an oil company then?"

"Oil company? Goodness me, no." The suggestion seemed to amuse the man. "You think Phillips was in oil, as it were?"

"Wasn't he?" Rich said.

"He was working with our dad," Jade told the man.

The man nodded. "That much is true, certainly."

"So you know who we are," Rich asked.

"Of course. And I'm delighted to meet you both. Did I say that already? Sorry if I didn't. And sorry about your mother too, by the way. Oh, and your father of course."

"Sorry doesn't help," Jade said.

"No," the man agreed. "Sorry."

If he meant this as a joke, he gave no sign of it. He glanced toward the kitchen. "I wonder if the kettle is still serviceable. I really could do with a cup of tea. It's been a very long night—and not a terribly productive one at that."

"Who are you?" Rich said, trying to sound calm and in control.

"Oh, I am so sorry." The man extended his hand and approached them. Then he realized that he was still holding the bloodstained handkerchief, and he stopped and let his hand drop. "My name is Ardman. My friends call me . . ." He frowned. "Actually, they call me Ardman too. Though I don't seem to have very many friends these days."

"All got shot, did they?" Jade said sarcastically.

Ardman turned away, looking back at the dead body on the floor. "Yes, actually. A fair few of them anyway." When he turned back he was smiling again. "Those men won't be back," he reassured them. "They've finished here. Now, why don't you make us some tea?" he said to Jade.

"Because I don't want any tea," Jade told him.

"Oh, that's a shame."

"And what do you want?" Rich demanded. "Apart from tea? Wouldn't be a sample of fuel oil, would it?"

Ardman's eyes narrowed. "Well, now that you mention it . . . I did think Phillips might have it on him, in the absence of your father. But sadly not."

"Look," Rich said, "we don't mean to be unfriendly, but who are you? What are you doing here?"

"As I said, my name is Ardman." He rubbed again at his hand with the handkerchief. "I work for what you might call the security services."

"MI5?" Rich said, looking at Jade. He was reminded again of Magda's words of warning.

"That sort of thing. But not exactly. Actually, I run a small and rather secret department that reports directly to a committee called COBRA. Maybe you've heard of that?"

"No," Rich said.

"Never mind, never mind. It's a committee chaired by the prime minister, or his appointed and anointed. The name sounds very exciting, but it's actually named after the place the committee meets—the Cabinet Office Briefing Rooms Annex."

"A committee?" Rich said in surprise.

". . . that meets in an annex?" Jade said.

"Well, it's a little more grand than that," Ardman said with a sniff. "And COBRA only meets in emergencies. Anything from hijackings to bombings to a shortage of water in the South East. My group tends not to be called in for the water shortages."

"And you've taken Dad," Jade said.

"Good gracious, no. But talking of water, I think I'll just run this under the tap, if you don't mind." He held up the handkerchief. "Don't want to stain my clothes."

"Don't want his blood on your hands," Jade retorted.

Ardman was already on his way to the kitchen. "Too late for that, I fear," he said sadly.

Rich grabbed Jade's hand and led her quickly across the room to the hall. He tried to move quietly, but their feet crunched on broken glass from the window.

Ardman turned and called after them from the kitchen door. "I'd like to talk to you, if I may."

"You may not," Jade told him. "You've taken Dad; you're not getting us."

"We didn't take your father," Ardman said, his voice suddenly hard-edged. The amiable banter was gone and he was staring at them intently. "Why would we do that? Think about it."

"We have," Rich said. He'd heard enough. There was nothing the man had said that made him want to trust Ardman—assuming that really was his name.

"We're not staying here to listen to your lies," Jade added. "Come on."

"You're in danger," Ardman's voice came after them. "You really should listen to what I have to say."

"We really should go," Jade hissed as Rich hesitated in the hallway.

Ardman was standing in the door to the living room, but he made no effort to follow them any farther.

"We can look after ourselves," Rich called to him.

"Maybe you can," Ardman agreed. "But whatever you do," he shouted after them as they left, "don't even think about going after Viktor Vishinsky on your own. That really would be dangerous."

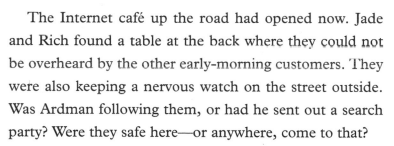

13

The Internet café up the road had opened now. Jade and Rich found a table at the back where they could not be overheard by the other early-morning customers. They were also keeping a nervous watch on the street outside. Was Ardman following them, or had he sent out a search party? Were they safe here—or anywhere, come to that?

"What was that name again?" Jade asked, still looking around anxiously.

"Viktor Vishinsky," Rich said. He had a good memory for facts and details. Something he had perhaps inherited from his father, he realized, remembering the way Chance immediately memorized their cell phone numbers.

Jade typed into the search field on the computer: *victor vishinski*. It came back a few moments later with a list of Web pages. Most of them were about someone called Victor but with a different surname. One was for a comic called The Victor. Some were about victors of sporting events. Not hopeful.

But at the top of the page there was a line of text:

"Did you mean *Viktor Vishinsky*?"

"Maybe we do," Rich said. "Try it."

The results this time were very different. There was a lot of information about Viktor Vishinsky.

"Look," Rich said, pointing to one of the first items in the list. "That's the KOS Web site. KOS was the oil company Magda mentioned." He clicked on it and they waited for the page to load.

"Maybe we should have stayed and talked," Rich said. "To Ardman, I mean."

"He was lying," Jade said. "They're all lying. Except maybe Magda. No one else has told us the truth since Mum died. Not even our own dad."

They examined the page. It was a company profile. KOS, it seemed, stood for Krejikistan Oil Subsidiaries, and Viktor Vishinsky owned and ran the company. There was a picture of him—a confident-looking man with hair that was almost white. He could be in his sixties or his late forties, it was difficult to tell.

"So what's he got to do with anything?" Jade wondered.

"If Magda's right, he's the guy that Dad was spying on," Rich said. "Here, look at this . . ." He had scrolled down and was now reading more about the company and the country where it was based.

"What?"

"Interesting, that's all. I've never heard of Krejikistan, but it looks like it was part of the Soviet Union before everything broke apart there. Now it's got its own government, but the economy is dominated by this one oil company—KOS."

"Do they have much oil there?" Jade wondered.

"None at all, from the look of it," Rich said, scrolling down the screen to a map of the country. The map showed a long thin country running down the western side of Russia. "Looks like it's the position that's important rather than what they actually have there." He read quickly through the text. "Yes, look at this. KOS makes almost all of its money by leasing pipelines so that oil can flow through the country."

"So everything has to come through Krejikistan."

Rich had finished skimming through the text. "Yep," he said. "If the Ukraine wants oil or gas from Russia, it has to pay for use of the pipeline it comes through. The same for any of Russia's customers—basically, the whole of western Europe. They pay by the barrel. Must cost a fortune."

"Bet they don't like that," Jade said.

"Bet they don't. But Krejikistan—or rather this KOS company—controls the whole thing. Pay through the nose, or ship everything miles and miles out of your way."

"Right," Jade agreed. "But that doesn't help us find Dad. Or help us understand why this Ardman bloke warned us not to mess with Vishinsky."

"I'll tell you something else I don't understand," Rich said.

"Yeah?"

"Why would the Ministry of Defense be doing business with a company that is owned and based in the former Soviet Union? And what does this KOS company have that they'd want anyway? Okay, look." He pointed at a list of KOS sites around the world. "They've got some sort of research facility and storage depot just outside London. But even so."

Jade looked where Rich was pointing. "Isn't that the place there was a big fire or something last week? I saw a headline, I'm sure." She leaned back in the hard café seat. "So what now? Phone a friend?" She pulled Dad's cell phone from her backpack.

They leaned close over the phone. It was switched on but key-locked. Rich managed to work out how to un-lock it, and they checked the address book. There were no numbers in it.

"Big help," Jade said.

Rich sighed. "He really is Johnny No-Mates. Hang on, there should be a list of calls made and received somewhere." He fiddled with the phone until he found the call register. "Here we are. Look—he's made a fair few calls. Received a load too, but all from 'Number Withheld.' Another big help."

The phone vibrated in Rich's hand.

"What did you do that for?" Jade asked.

"I didn't."

"Someone calling?"

The phone had stopped. Rich showed Jade the screen. "One Text Message Received."

"Let's have a look then," she said.

The message read: "Is sample safe? Do you have it? Where?? Urgent you reply. Dad."

"Thank God he's safe!" Jade said.

"Is he?" Rich wondered.

"What do you mean? He sent us a text."

Rich took the phone back from Jade and read the text message again. "But we've got his phone. And why did he send it to himself?" Rich pulled his own cell from his pocket. "Did you get the message too? I didn't. Easy enough to send all the phones the same text."

"Are you saying this didn't come from Dad?" Jade asked. "Then who did send it?"

"Someone who wants this sample everyone keeps going on about. Whatever it is. But who?" Rich was working the buttons. "Probably number withheld again," he muttered. "Whoa! Here we go. They have to give us the number so we can reply." The number that came up in the text message details was so long it wrapped onto a second line of the screen. "Is that a cell number?" he wondered out loud.

"You going to call back?" Jade wondered.

"Not till I know more about it. And not from this phone." He turned back to the computer keyboard and typed the first digits of the number into the Internet search page.

"Here you are, look. It's an international dialing code."

"Don't tell me," Jade said as Rich scrolled to it.

"Krejikistan," they said in unison.

"Right. Doesn't mean the phone is there, though," Rich said. "But that's where they got the phone and that's where they pay the bills."

"You going to call the number? Can't be any harm in calling, can there?"

"Except then they'll know we have the phone, and we got the message. I don't know about you, Jade, but I think the more we keep to ourselves the better. I mean, it's not like we're going to Krejikistan, is it?"

A group of armed soldiers took John Chance at gunpoint from the plane, his hands still tied. A car was waiting—a big black limo with tinted windows. But they put Chance in a jeep driven by a soldier. Two more soldiers got in the back. One of them grinned and aimed his rifle at Chance. The soldier had a tooth missing and the ones he had left were going gray.

"It's amazing what money can buy," Chance said cheerily. "Limousines, private jets, the services of your country's armed forces. Good dental work."

The soldier jabbed Chance with the rifle and shouted at him in Russian to be quiet.

Chance pretended not to understand and got shouted at again before the driver said, "No speak."

"Why didn't you say?" Chance told him and settled himself down for a long journey.

It seemed to be a military airfield, with a high perimeter fence and soldiers on patrol. The barrier at the main gate was opened for the limo ahead of them, and it didn't even slow down. But the jeep had to stop to allow the driver to shout at the gate guards.

"So where are we going?" Chance asked as they turned onto a narrow road and headed away from the air base.

"No speak," the driver said again.

"Is that far?"

The driver glared. Chance smiled back. They continued in silence. Once they reached the main roads, there were signs. They were in Russian, but Chance could read them well enough and he had a good idea where they were headed. Sure enough, after less than an hour, they turned off the main road onto a service road that led to a massive industrial complex on the horizon.

"Krejikistan Oil Subsidiaries," Chance said out loud. "Do they fly a flag when Vishinsky is in residence, or does he live somewhere else?"

"No speak," the driver shouted above the sound of the

engine. He pointed through the windshield at the complex ahead as if there might be some doubt where they were heading.

Once he was through the gates and into Vishinsky's complex, Chance thought, there would be very little hope he'd ever get out again. At least, not alive. So he smiled at the driver and nodded to show he had understood. Then he hurled himself sideways.

Chance's shoulder slammed into the driver, knocking him into the side of the jeep. The man's hands came off the steering wheel and the jeep lurched off the narrow strip of road onto the dry mud of the verge. The jeep bumped and jolted and the two soldiers in the backseat struggled to bring their rifles to bear.

But Chance had been expecting it. He braced himself against the steering wheel so that the driver couldn't get control back. His hands were lashed together at the wrist, so he laced his fingers together and using both hands as a single fist, thumped the driver hard in the face. The jeep's door burst open and the driver tumbled out.

One of the soldiers behind Chance had recovered enough to bring his rifle up. Chance propelled himself upward, pushing hard on the jeep's floor with his feet. He twisted and shouldered into the rifle as it went off. Then he head-butted the soldier, who collapsed back into the rear seat. The jeep lurched as the bullet tore into the engine. There was a grating of tortured metal and the vehicle began to slow as it careered across the uneven ground and came to a stop.

The second soldier was young, probably not yet out of his teens. He sat frozen as Chance turned toward him. His rifle was hanging from his shaking hands. Chance thrust his fists at the boy.

"Untie me!" he said in Russian.

His words seemed to bring the soldier back to reality, and he struggled out of the jeep and ran. His rifle fell forgotten to the ground.

Chance watched the figure receding into the distance, passing the driver lying motionless beside the road. Chance knew he didn't have long before the lad raised the alarm. And he was stuck in the middle of nowhere with his hands tied and with a wrecked jeep.

The soldier in the backseat, the one Chance had head-butted, groaned and muttered something. Chance bunched his fists together again and swung hard. The soldier slumped back, unconscious.

"No speak," Chance said.

14

The café was busier by mid-morning. Rich and Jade spoke quietly so as not to be overheard by the people at nearby tables. They had decided not to call the number in Krejikistan, but now they were not sure what they could do.

"Maybe we should try the number he kept calling," Rich said.

"He didn't keep calling it," Jade told him.

"He called it more than he called anyone else," Rich

pointed out. "In fact, he didn't call anyone else. Ever. Not on this phone." He sighed. "You got any better ideas?"

Jade had to admit she didn't. "Just see who answers. If anyone. Probably more voice mail."

Rich held the phone so they could both hear. The numbers beeped through as the phone dialed. Then they heard the ringing at the other end. It seemed to ring for ages, and Rich was about to give up when the phone was finally answered.

"Hello?" a voice said. It sounded slightly tentative, as if whoever was speaking had been surprised to get the call. "This is Andrew Phillips's phone."

Their faces were close together, hunched over the phone, and Rich saw Jade's eyes widen. Rich hung up, almost dropping the phone like it was hot.

"Phillips," he said. "The man who . . ." He swallowed, his throat dry.

"The man who was shot," Jade completed for him, whispering, looking around to make sure no one was listening. But nobody seemed at all interested in the two children sitting in the back corner of the café close to the bathrooms.

"So who's answering his phone?" Rich said.

"Friend, colleague, whatever. Question is—do we trust them?"

Rich thought about this. "Do no harm to talk to them. Phillips was shot; he tried to protect us. He was a friend of Dad's. Probably."

"Probably," Jade agreed. "Try it."

But before Rich got the chance, the phone rang, vibrating on the table between them.

"Can cell phone calls be traced?" Jade whispered as though the phone might hear them.

"Doubt it," Rich said. "There's no line, is there? You'd need, like, a satellite or something. They just did 1471 to get our number and called back." He took a deep breath and answered the phone.

It was a different voice this time. A familiar voice.

"I'm guessing that is either Jade or Rich," the voice said. "You remember we met this morning?"

"It's both of us," Rich said.

"Please don't hang up. I think we need to talk, though I do appreciate you must be feeling a little vulnerable right now."

"Vulnerable?" Jade was making an effort to keep her voice down. "Men being shot dead. Dad kidnapped. Killers after us. Yeah, just a bit, I'd say."

"Understandable," the voice agreed. "And I really do want to help you. In fact, I may be the only person who can."

"We've heard that before," Rich said. "But how do we know you're telling the truth? How do we know we can trust you?"

"You can trust me," Ardman said. "Really you can." His voice was controlled, reassuring, confident. Jade and

Rich looked into each other's eyes as they tried to decide if he was telling the truth.

Ardman was sitting at Phillips's bare desk as he spoke into the phone. On the other side of the office, a man was gesturing to Ardman to keep talking. Rich and Jade could be heard through speakers attached to the phone.

But they were not the only things attached to the phone. There was another wire that led to a powerful computer where a third man—a technician—was working rapidly.

"It's Chance's cell phone all right," he said, just loud enough for Ardman to hear. "Issued by us, so I'm activating the global positioning tracker now. It'll be online so long as they keep the connection open. Lose the call and you lose them."

"Do we have a satellite in position?" the man who had gestured to Ardman asked, equally quietly.

"Patching through to a US Department of Defense bird," the technician said. "It'll take them hours to realize they've lost control. Then they'll blame the techies. Or the hardware."

"How long?" Ardman mouthed at the man. Into the phone he said, "Just listen to what I have to say, that's all I ask. Where's the possible harm in that, hmmm?"

"Almost in," the technician said. "Accessing now. Should have a fix for you in about a minute." He turned the screen so that Ardman could see the image on it.

It was a map of Britain. A rectangle appeared over the lower half, and the image changed to show just the area in that rectangle. Then another as the image zoomed in again—on London. With every second, the satellite closed in on the location of Chance's cell phone . . .

"Got the general location," the technician observed. "I'll get a team into the area ready. I think it's Goddard on standby today. Soon as we have a street address—bingo!" He grinned. "Shouldn't be long now."

In Krejikistan, the Commander was sitting in the passenger seat of a heavy truck as it made its way along the narrow track from the KOS main facility. He had waited perhaps longer than he should have for the jeep, and it wasn't just the bumping of the vehicle that was making him feel queasy. He knew what would happen if he had lost Vishinsky's "guest."

The sight of a soldier staggering along the narrow service road toward them, waving his arms to flag them down, did nothing to ease the Commander's fears.

"Private Levin, sir. I was escorting the English prisoner," the soldier explained as soon as the truck stopped.

The Commander listened to Levin's story with increasing apprehension. As soon as he had the gist of it, he ordered the soldier to squeeze into the front of the truck with him and the driver. The heavy army truck then continued slowly along the access road until it came to the point where the jeep had careered off into the wilderness.

The tire tracks were easily visible in the mud even before Levin's enthusiastic shouts of: "Here—this is the place, sir. We'll find him now."

"I don't like the look of the mud," the driver said as he stopped the truck. "We could sink right in and be stuck here. A jeep's one thing, but in this . . ." He shrugged and waited for the Commander to make the decision.

The Commander shoved Levin out of the truck. Then he ordered the troops in the back to get out and follow the tire tracks. Private Levin was still insisting the prisoner could not have gone far and that they would soon find him—right up until they found another unconscious soldier.

"I want that jeep found," the Commander ordered as soon as the unconscious soldier had been carried back to the truck. "Private Levin says it was damaged, stopped. So it's close by somewhere."

It did not take long to find it—with yet another unconscious soldier in the back. There was no sign of their former prisoner apart from the ropes his hands had been tied with—sliced through on the ragged metal of the jeep's hood and dropped nearby.

The soldier in the jeep was coming around. He seemed groggy. He insisted he was fine to help with the search, but the Commander sent him back to the truck.

"Take him and the other one back to the KOS facility in the truck," he ordered. "Get them checked out by the medics there."

One of the soldiers helped the groggy man out of the

jeep and back toward the truck. The man still seemed to be suffering, head down and face in shadow.

The Commander walked back to where Levin was standing, staring out into the empty wilderness. "You will stay and help us find the prisoner you lost," the Commander said. "He can't have gone far. Search parties—groups of two or three," he ordered. "Spread out from this point, on the double. What are you waiting for?"

Within a few minutes, there was a shout from one of the search parties. They had found the man dressed in civilian clothes lying dead in a gully.

"Looks like he fell and knocked himself out," one of the soldiers who had found him said. It was several minutes before the Commander thought to have Levin look at the unconscious man to be sure.

The private stared in amazement.

"The prisoner?" the Commander prompted. "Yes?"

Levin shook his head. "No."

"So who is he?" the Commander demanded.

"It's Dimitri. He was with me in the back of the jeep."

"Why isn't he in uniform?"

"He was," Levin protested. "Those are the prisoner's clothes."

The Commander frowned. "And Dimitri was in the back of the jeep? But we have just taken that man to the truck. So where is . . ." His mouth dropped open and he grabbed his radio.

• • •

The truck pulled into the main compound, surrounded by industrial units—metal-clad buildings, pipelines, pumping stations. Smoke billowed out from vents and valves so that it was like emerging from the back of the truck into some region of hell itself.

Chance made a play of rubbing his head. "Sick bay," he grunted, hoping the guards now carrying the soldier from the truck wouldn't notice his accent needed some work.

They didn't seem bothered and Chance suppressed a smile. He had hoped to be able to walk away, on the pretext of helping with the search for himself. With luck, he had reckoned he could get to the main road and flag down a lift—maybe even commandeer a car and head for the Ukrainian border.

But instead he had been escorted right into the heart of enemy territory—right to the place they'd been taking him anyway. To Chance's mind it was a setback, not a defeat. There would be a vehicle somewhere he could "borrow."

He turned from the tailgate of the truck. And found himself staring into the barrel of a rifle. Three soldiers stood in front of him, all aiming their weapons. A fourth was listening to his radio.

"It is all right," the fourth soldier said into the handset. "We have him now."

Chance sighed. "It was worth a try," he said. "You've got to grant me that." He put his hands in the air. "Coming quietly," he said in Russian, adding in quiet English, "For now."

"We need to meet," Ardman's voice said from the other end of the phone. "We can't do this over the phone."

"You mean, so you can have us arrested, or shot, or whatever?" Jade said. She looked at Rich, and could tell from his expression that he agreed with her—it was too risky.

"I understand you must be wary."

"Terrified, more like," Jade muttered. Rich smiled.

"So," Ardman went on, not having heard, "why don't you choose the place and the time. I promise to come alone. Just me. Choose somewhere public, somewhere you can tell if you're being watched, where you can escape easily if you think you're in trouble. But I promise you, that won't be necessary. Really it won't."

"Hang on," Jade said, covering the phone with her hand. "What do you think?" she asked Rich quietly.

Rich shrugged. "What else can we do? And like he says, we can choose somewhere they wouldn't dare try anything."

"We hope," Jade said. "All right, where?"

"Here?"

"Too crowded. We need somewhere we can talk. Safely. Anyway, we might want to come back here, use the computers or whatever. So it's best they don't know about this place. But a café or restaurant or bar or somewhere might be good."

Rich grinned suddenly. "What about the bar in a big hotel? He pays."

"We're not drinking," Jade said. "Clear heads—right?"

"I meant a Coke," Rich said. "Or maybe lunch."

Ardman's voice came from the phone as Jade removed her hand. "Are you still there?"

"We're here," she assured him. "Name me three big hotels in Central London. Just any three. First you think of."

Ardman did so, though he sounded puzzled. "The Savoy, the Ritz, the Clarendorf?"

"The last one. The Clarendorf." Jade raised her eyebrows at Rich—a question. He nodded. It would do. "We'll meet you in the main bar. In half an hour. If we're not there, wait for us. See you." She made to end the call.

"Hang on," Ardman said quickly.

Jade hesitated. "What?"

"If you don't recognize me—"

"We will," Rich said.

"Just in case. I'll leave my name with the barman, so he knows where I am. Just ask for Hilary Ardman."

Rich laughed out loud.

"What's funny?" Ardman asked, sounding a bit hurt.

"Hilary's a girl's name," Jade said.

"And Jade is a slippery semiprecious stone," the man snapped back. "I'll see you in half an hour."

The technician was giving a thumbs-up. Ardman nodded and put down the phone.

"Got 'em," the technician said.

Ardman swung his feet off the desk and stood up. He took his jacket off the back of the chair and slipped it on.

"Coming to see the fun?" the third man in the room asked. He had just finished speaking urgently into his own cell phone.

"No," Ardman told him. "I'm off to the Clarendorf for a drink."

The man laughed. "Right." Then he realized that Ardman was not laughing. "You're serious? They won't be there, will they?"

"We'll see," Ardman said. "If Goddard's people underestimate these kids, then I'd rather we had a backup. We can't let Vishinsky get to them."

"If Goddard's team loses them, they're not likely to come and find you, are they?" the man said.

But Ardman had gone.

"Do we meet him?" Jade wondered.

"I still don't trust him, whatever he says," Rich told her.

"Me neither," she agreed. "So, what do we do? Go and see if he turns up, then decide if we see him?"

"I've got an idea," Rich said. "How much power's that phone got left in it?"

Jade pulled the cell back out of her backpack. "Looks like—"

There was a sudden squeal of brakes from outside the

café. At the same moment, it sounded like a hundred emergency sirens had started up. Through the window, Jade and Rich could both see several police cars screeching to a halt in the road outside. Two of them veered sideways at opposite sides of the café, blocking off the road.

Car doors opened and uniformed police leaped out. But even before they reached the café, the door crashed violently open. Men in dark suits and darker glasses rushed inside.

"Armed officers—nobody move!"

15

As soon as he heard the first car screech to a halt outside, Rich was on his feet. He grabbed Jade and bundled her ahead of him through the nearby door that led to the bathrooms at the back of the café.

"I thought the police weren't interested," Jade gasped.

"That was then," Rich said. "This is now."

As well as two doors into the bathrooms, there was a third door. It had a bar across it and a fire exit sign above. Rich shoved the bar and felt it give. The door was stiff through lack of use, but with Jade's help he managed to heave it open.

"How did they find us?" she asked. "Ardman?"

"He doesn't know where we are."

"Are you sure?"

"Maybe they traced the call somehow," Rich conceded. He was looking around, deciding where to go next.

They were in a courtyard area at the back of the café. There was another door back into the kitchens, and a gate that had to open into the street beyond for deliveries. Large, round, industrial-sized metal garbage cans stood grouped in a corner. Rich didn't fancy trying to hide inside those.

He heaved open the gate and looked out into the road beyond. "It won't take them long to guess where we went."

"Assuming they know we were actually there," Jade said.

There was a big key in the lock of the gate. Jade pulled it out, and when she closed the gate behind them, she locked it shut. It was solid wood, like a barn door, so you couldn't see through.

"Should keep them guessing," she said.

The street outside was a dead end, finishing at a wall. The other end of the street joined the main road at the front of the café, and they made their way cautiously toward the junction.

Behind them, Rich could hear the gates rattling as someone tried to open them from the other side. With luck they'd assume no one could have gotten out. They might go and ask for the key, but that would take time.

Rich and Jade emerged into the main street beyond the area blocked by the two sideways police cars. But farther down the road, several policemen were setting up a barrier of plastic tape.

"We're trapped," Jade said. "Bet it's the same the other end of the road."

"They can't just close the road forever."

"They won't. They'll close it off, then search for us."

"Side street," Rich decided. "If we're quick, they won't have cordoned them all off."

There was a side street between the dead end they had come from and the cordon. They tried to look inconspicuous, hoping the police wouldn't look down the street and see them as they hurried along the sidewalk. Luckily, the police at the barrier were busy answering questions and taking flack from people who wanted to come through.

Rich and Jade slipped onto the side street. There were houses down one side of it. A brick wall ran along the other side—too high to climb. A row of tall, mature trees was planted along the side where the wall was, between the road and the sidewalk.

"Maybe go through one of the houses?" Jade said. "Get out the back door and through the garden."

"If they have one," Rich said. "If we don't get trapped

inside. If whoever opens the door to us doesn't just shout for the police. Yeah, great plan."

As they hastened along the street, they could now see the uniformed figure standing at the other end, turning people away.

"It may be the only plan we have," Jade said. "What else can we do? Hide up a tree?"

Rich hadn't thought of that. Okay, so his sister was joking, but maybe . . . He looked up at the nearest tree by the side of the road. To be honest, he doubted they'd be very hidden, even if they managed to get up into the branches.

"Jade, Rich," a voice said from behind them. "How nice to see you again so soon."

Spinning around, tensed and ready to run, Rich was surprised to see the figure standing behind them. It was the woman from the café. She must have followed them from the main street. She wore a long gray raincoat and carried a large black handbag under her arm as if it were heavy. Her long black hair blew slightly in the breeze.

"You called the police!" Jade accused her.

"I certainly did not," she assured them. "I think we should get away from here as quickly as possible."

"You'll help us escape?"

"Stay here," she said, smiling. "I'll tell the policeman at the end that I saw two suspicious-looking children going into one of the gardens. When he goes to see, you can get past. I'll keep the policeman busy as long as I can and meet you in the next road. There is a post office and newsstand. Wait for me in there."

"What if we're spotted?" Rich said.

"You won't be. Trust me." Magda nodded and smiled. "You have been through so much, you poor children. Let me help you. Let me help you and everything will be all right—you'll see."

Rich looked at Jade. Jade was nodding in agreement. "All right," she said. "I think we need all the help we can get." She smiled, but it was a smile full of sadness. "Thank you."

Magda smiled back. "My pleasure. Now, be ready."

While Magda went up to the policeman, Rich and Jade kept to the shadows close to the high wall and under one of the large trees at the side of the road. They watched Magda talk to the policeman, who seemed very keen to follow such an attractive woman to the gate into the garden of the house at the end of the street.

"Men," Jade said.

"What do you mean?" Rich said. "If he hadn't gone with her, we'd be stuck here."

They ran quickly and quietly to the end of the road and ducked around the corner. They stopped to get their breath back beside the hedge—the hedge around the garden of the house on the end. The policeman was probably right on the other side, but the hedge was tall and dense, so there was no chance of him seeing them.

"That post office must be just along here," Jade said.

"Yes," Rich agreed. "Lucky Magda found us when she did." He wondered whether she'd been looking for them or whether it was pure luck. He was about to follow Jade along the road when there was a strange popping sound from the other side of the hedge.

"What was that?" he asked, careful to keep his voice down.

Jade ran back to see what he wanted. "I didn't hear anything," she said. But even as she spoke, the sound came again—twice more in rapid succession.

"They having a champagne party?" Jade wondered.

Rich could see a part of the hedge where it was quite thin—more twigs and branches than leaves. He reached his arms in between the thin branches and pulled them apart in the hope of seeing through, into the garden on the other side. Jade leaned in close beside him, also looking through the gap Rich had made.

They had a good view of a well-kept lawn bordered with neatly weeded flower beds. But that was not what made Rich and Jade freeze with sudden horror.

The policeman was lying on his back on the ground. Magda was standing over him. She was holding a pistol with a long chunky silencer aimed down at the policeman's dead body. And there was no doubt in Rich's numbed mind that the man was dead. He could see the sightless staring eyes, the frozen look of fear and the smoking hole in the man's forehead . . .

Magda checked the gun and slipped it inside her bag. Then she looked up as if sensing that she was being watched. Looked straight at the gap in the hedge where Rich and Jade were staring back at her.

Jade recovered from the shock before Rich did. She grabbed her brother's arm. "Run!" she hissed.

And together, they ran.

16

The main bar of the Clarendorf Hotel was subtly lit even in the middle of the day. It was a long narrow room in the Regency building, with leather sofas and armchairs arranged around polished wooden tables.

At one end was the bar, with its oak-paneled front matching the walls of the room and its polished marble top gleaming. At the other end of the long room was a small gallery, reached by a narrow staircase in the foyer that led to the back of the gallery. There were several more tables on the balcony, but today only one of them was occupied. A man and a woman arrived soon after Ardman and sipped at their drinks, almost hidden in the shadows at the back.

Ardman spared them only a glance as he looked around for any sign of Rich and Jade. He was a few minutes early, and if Goddard was as good as he liked to think he was, then the twins would already be safely in the back of an unmarked car.

He found himself an armchair from which he could watch both doors into the bar and have a good view of the other patrons—not that there were many—and gestured to the bartender that he'd like a drink.

The bartender came and took his order for a cup of Earl Grey tea. It was a bit early in the day for anything more, Ardman decided. But if he was here for the duration, then a single malt would help ease the boredom later. The bartender returned with the tea—in a small silver-plated teapot together with bone china teacup and saucer and a silver jug of milk.

The sugar was crystalized, like little uncut precious stones in a china bowl. Amused, Ardman selected two crystals that were pale green like unpolished jade and dropped them into his tea.

When his phone rang, Ardman checked the display on the screen and then answered: "Hello, Mr. Goddard. You are calling with good news, I hope?"

Goddard sounded embarrassed. "I can't think how we missed them."

Ardman sighed. "It happens. Don't worry. And I've met these kids, albeit briefly. They're good. Very good, it seems."

He could almost hear Goddard shuffling uneasily at the other end of the call. "There is one other unfortunate piece of bad news, sir."

Ardman listened, his face grave. "That is unfortunate," he agreed. "I doubt if the Chance twins did it, but I'll take care . . ."

"I think you should have backup, sir," Goddard said.

"No, no, I certainly don't want your people stomping all over this place with their heavy boots. You've frightened them off once, I don't want you doing it again."

"You think they'll turn up?"

"I don't know," Ardman said. "But it's the only hope we have—the only hope they have, for that matter. So I shall wait all day if I have to."

Rich watched Ardman for a while from the doorway before he plucked up the courage to go over. He and Jade had been watching the man since he arrived. Now Rich was sure the man had seen him, but he went on drinking his tea as if nothing had changed. It was hard to get the image of the man wiping blood onto a handkerchief out of his mind. But then Rich remembered the sight of Magda standing over the dead policeman, smoking gun still in her hand. He shivered, and walked quickly across to where Ardman was sitting.

"Just you?" Ardman asked as Rich sat down opposite him in another of the leather armchairs. Rich took out his cell phone and put it on the table between them.

"Jade's listening. You don't need to know where she is. She could be miles away. Any sign of trouble and she's gone."

Ardman nodded. "Very good. You're assuming I want both of you and of course you're right. But I want to make sure you're safe."

"Did you send the police?"

Ardman didn't answer. "Was it you who killed PC Skinner?" he asked instead.

Rich felt his mouth go dry. "No," he said. "It was the woman, Magda. Is she one of your lot?"

Ardman shook his head. "Definitely not. Though if the lady in question has long black hair, then we certainly have a file on her. Beautiful but deadly. You'd be well advised to keep out of her way."

"Thanks, but I think we worked that out for ourselves," Rich said. He nodded at the phone on the table between them. "You've got about ten minutes before my credit runs out. Then I'm leaving."

"Your father works for me," Ardman said. "He's a government agent, for want of a better term. As I told you, I run a rather special department reporting to the Cabinet Office emergencies committee COBRA. Or certain people who serve on it, at any rate."

"And what does our dad do for you?" Rich wanted to know. "Apart from get abducted?"

"In this case, he was keeping tabs on an oil company."

"KOS."

Ardman nodded. "That's right. He took the place of an industry expert called Lessiter."

"We know. What happened to Lessiter?"

"He was delighted to find that before taking up the post he had the chance for a free cruise around the Mediterranean with his family, and all at Her Majesty's taxpayers' expense."

Rich frowned. "He's not dead then?"

Ardman looked shocked. "Please, what sort of man do you think I am?"

"I'm not sure you want me to answer that."

Ardman smiled. "Touché. Would you like a drink, by the way?"

"No thanks. I'm not staying."

"Still not convinced?" Ardman sounded disappointed. "What else can I tell you then? Let me see . . . I needed a man on the inside at KOS to see what Vishinsky was up to. He's—"

"We know who Viktor Vishinsky is."

"Good, that will save time. Then you'll know that I needed absolute proof there was a . . . what shall we say? A problem?" He nodded as if agreeing with his own choice of word. "That there was a problem before I could act against KOS officially."

"Why?"

For the first time Ardman seemed irritated. "Because

Vishinsky is a rich and powerful man with friends in high places. I had hoped you would find that out when I let his name slip for you."

"It was deliberate?" Rich asked in surprise.

Ardman looked at him with sympathy. "Young man," he said, "you need to realize that in this game, the game you're now in, everything is deliberate." He paused to pour himself more tea before going on. "Vishinsky knows that too. And it is not by chance that he is so friendly with many powerful people in this country as well as others in Europe and the US. It is quite deliberate that he knows our own prime minister so well—and that he has had him to stay on holiday at the Vishinsky villa in Italy."

"So you sent our dad to get the dirt on him?"

"I wouldn't phrase it quite like that myself," Ardman said. "But, yes. In a nutshell."

"And it went wrong."

"Yes," Ardman said again. "Vishinsky is planning something, but only your father, and possibly not even him, knows what it is. Your father and a . . . colleague managed to get into a secure laboratory facility at the KOS installation just outside London. They removed a sample of fluid. But what that fluid is, why it is important and where it is now, we don't know."

"Magda mentioned a sample of fuel."

"Perhaps she knows its significance. If we can find it, we can analyze it and discover what it is. From that we can make a good guess what it might be for. Your father had it hidden until he could pass it on safely to his contact, another of my men. Andrew Phillips."

"The man who was shot in the apartment."

Ardman nodded. "Maybe he passed it on and Phillips hid it or it was taken from him. But if this Magda woman is asking about it, then the sample must still be hidden." He fixed his eyes firmly on Rich. "It is very important that I get that sample of fuel," he said solemnly. "Do you know where it is?"

Rich shivered under the intense stare. "Where's Dad?" he countered. He didn't want to admit to knowing—or not knowing—anything. Not yet.

"I'm afraid that Vishinsky has taken him. He too is desperate to recover the sample, probably to stop us getting it. Though it is possible he needs it back."

"Why? He must have loads of the stuff."

Ardman smiled. "Possibly. But there was a bit of an incident at his London facility. Just after your father left. As you may have heard—the whole place blew up. An accident, of course."

Rich shivered again. "Dad?"

"Your father," Ardman said, leaning forward so that the phone on the table between them got it loud and clear, "is a very brave man. But he's on his own now and in terrible danger. I'm asking you to help me help him. Please."

The door to the gallery area overlooking the bar was closed. Anyone going up the narrow staircase to the gallery would have found a notice on the door that said: CLOSED FOR REN-OVATION. Returning to the bar and looking up, they might have thought it was odd, then, that there were two people sitting up there.

The man and the woman in the gallery did not think it odd at all. It was Stabb who had stuck the notice on the door. Now he and Magda were leaning close over the table between them.

They were listening to the voices coming through single earpieces, connected by a thin wire to a device taped to one of the ornate wooden struts at the front of the balcony. A powerful directional microphone pointed straight at Ardman and Rich, sitting halfway down the bar, a cell phone on the table between them.

". . . help me help him. Please." Ardman's voice was slightly tinny but it was clear enough.

"Oh, how sweet of the man," Magda said, pushing her long black hair behind her ear. "Wanting to help the poor little boy. Should we offer to help him too, do you think?"

Stabb shook his head. "We need them both. Chance doesn't seem to care about them, so we can't use the brats to put pressure on him. But if we have them both, we can threaten one to make the other tell us where the sample is hidden. The security services know nothing, it seems, so Mr. Vishinsky can go ahead. Nothing can stop him now. Just as soon as we get those kids."

17

The hotel lobby was large and impersonal. There was a big seating area off to one side, close to the main bar. Jade had found a high-backed chair where she could sit without being seen by the staff at the reception desk. She had angled the chair so that it was facing a large fireplace.

There was no fire burning and she wasn't interested in the ornate fireplace itself. She was watching the mirror above the mantelpiece—in which she could see the reflected images of Rich and Ardman. She couldn't see

Ardman's face, so she was pretty sure that he could not see her—even if he was looking.

She and Rich had sat together here for a while, each trying in their own way to come to terms with what they had seen. They watched Ardman carefully, looking all around to check that the man really was alone. So far as they could tell, he had brought no one with him. When they were as sure as they could be, Rich called Jade's cell phone on Dad's and went to join Ardman in the bar.

Now Jade was listening intently to the conversation between her brother and the man from MI5, or whatever it was. Their voices were quiet and she had to strain to hear, even with the phone volume up full.

"There is something I think you should hear," Ardman was saying.

"Better be short," Rich told him. "I'm out of here any minute now."

"It won't take long. I have it on an MP3 file, which I understand is the way these things are done these days."

"Great, going to let me copy it onto my iPod, are you?" Rich said.

"I thought I'd play it on this, actually," Ardman replied. "If I put it here by the phone, then Jade can hear it as well. I assume that's okay?"

"Yeah, fine, whatever."

There was a pause, and in the mirror Jade could see Ardman reaching down to put something on the table between himself and Rich. She guessed it was a digital recorder from which he'd play back the file so they could hear.

"What you're about to hear," Ardman said, "is covered by the Official Secrets Act." He paused and Jade could almost hear him smiling. "Not that it makes much difference, but legally I have to tell you that."

"Covering yourself?"

"I like to do things properly. Now, this is a recording of a telephone conversation made last week. I'm not permitted to tell you who is speaking or why the conversation was recorded. But I think you'll recognize the voices and you'll guess why the gentleman's calls were all recorded. May I begin?"

"Get on with it," Rich told him.

Jade pressed the phone even harder against her ear, wondering what she was about to hear. When the recording started it was louder than the voices of Rich and Ardman, and she could actually hear it quite clearly.

The first voice said just one word: "Yes?" But Jade knew the voice at once—it was her father's.

"Is that Mr. Chance?" a woman's voice asked—tentative and slightly nervous.

"How did you get this number?" Chance demanded.

"Oh, dear," the woman said. "They did tell me this might be more difficult than . . . I got it from, er, well, your employers. I think. They were a bit vague at the Ministry when I—"

Chance cut her off. "What do you want?"

"My name is—"

Her name was obscured by a high-pitched bleep. Jade grimaced and pulled the phone from her ear, but she had recognized Mrs. Gilpin. Hesitating, she put it back, in time to hear Ardman's voice say quietly, "Sorry about that."

Mrs. Gilpin's voice went on. "I have some news for you, Mr. Chance. It's not good, I'm afraid. And . . . well, it may be a bit of a shock too. Are you sitting down, may I ask? I think perhaps you should."

"I'm used to bad news. And shocks. Just tell me."

"If you're sure. It's about Sandra, Sandra Chance."

There was a pause, and then Chance said slowly, "Go on. I'm sitting down."

"There's been an accident. A road accident. It was—there was nothing anyone could do. She didn't feel anything, it was instant. I . . . I'm sorry, I'm not doing this very well."

"You're doing fine. Thank you for letting me know. But it's been a long time since I last saw Sandra."

"But, the thing is—"

"Thank you," Chance insisted. Jade could hear the pent-up emotion in his voice. It might have been a long time, but he was feeling it. She knew exactly how he must have felt. It seemed like ages since they had come to the school and taken Rich and herself out of class to tell them . . . Hearing it again, Jade wiped her eyes with her free hand and wondered if Rich was all right. His image in the mirror seemed blurred and indistinct.

"I'm sure you have lots of other people you need to inform," Chance was saying stiffly. "Friends, family . . ."

"Er, no, actually," the woman said. "There's no one else. No one but you. I don't think she ever . . . Well, that's not for me to say. But I thought you should know straightaway. About Sandra I mean, but also that . . ."

"That what?"

"Well, that your children are fine. They weren't involved."

"My . . . children?"

"They've taken it very badly of course, but they're okay. They're good kids. Tough. They'll be all right. Only, well . . ."

"My children?" Chance said again. Jade could imagine him wondering what the hell was going on, what he was being told. After all these years.

"The funeral is tomorrow," the woman was saying. "I'm sorry it's not much warning, but it did take a long time to find you. Sandra left a letter that indicated you worked for the Civil Service. It was quite difficult tracking you down. . . . But if you can get here, I'm sure Rich and Jade will appreciate it."

There was silence from the other side of the call, so the woman went on.

"Your children need their father more than ever now. They need you, Mr. Chance."

Jade felt the tears in her eyes as she watched the blurred

image of Ardman lean forward in the mirror. The recording stopped with a click.

Rich sat frozen, all thoughts of leaving gone from his mind. In front of him, Ardman was selecting another file on the tiny personal MP3 player.

"This is rather more recent," he was saying. "Again, I can't tell you who the people are, but suffice it to say that one is the same man as on the previous recording, and the other man you have also met, albeit briefly. He is now, sadly, deceased."

"Phillips," Rich muttered.

If Ardman heard him, he gave no sign. "I'm sorry to have to do this to you," he said. "To both of you."

"I think I'm being watched," Chance's voice said from the device.

"You sure?" another voice asked. Rich recognized it immediately as Phillips's—though he sounded understandably calmer and less stressed than when Rich and Jade had met him.

"No. They're good, whoever they are. But it's even more urgent I get the sample to you."

"Yes, well, you were supposed to do that the other day and you never showed."

"I had to go to a funeral."

There was a pause, then Phillips said, "I heard. I'm sorry. I heard about the kids too—they okay?"

"Do you mean are they coping? Or am I coping?"

There was a short laugh. "Both, I suppose."

"Then, they're okay. They've gone out for the morning. God knows what I'll do with them when they get back. I need to sort out schools. It's a mess."

"A real pain, right? Something you could do without."

Chance's reply was surprisingly sharp. "I didn't mean it's messing me up. It's them I'm worried about. What sort of father am I? What sort of mess am I making for them? Their mum's just died and their world's turned upside down and what am I doing to help? I don't even know where to start."

"Yeah . . . Well, I'm sure you'll do your best."

"And what if that isn't good enough? These are my kids we're talking about. And the best I can do is to try and get them out of the way until it's safe to look after them properly. Have you any idea how that makes me feel? Have you?"

Rich was sitting openmouthed as he listened. It sounded like John Chance, but what he was saying seemed so at odds with how he and Jade had imagined he felt.

"Look, John," Phillips said, "I have to get this sample from you. We need to get it analyzed and find out what Vishinsky is up to. I'll come over this evening. Better when it's dark. When the kids are asleep."

"No," Chance said. "Not here."

"You really think the flat's being watched?"

"I can't take that risk."

"Safer at the flat than anywhere else, though."

"For you and me maybe," Chance agreed. "But not for my children. I can't risk them getting involved. I'm not putting them at risk, not at all, not for myself or you or anyone. Got that?"

Phillips seemed to sense Chance's determination. "Okay. Whatever you say. Look . . . I'll call later and we can discuss a good meeting place. You . . . do whatever you have to do."

"Thanks. I don't know really where to start. But that's it, isn't it? A new start. When I went up to Sandra's funeral, I had no idea. I mean—they told me there were two children, twins, and they're mine and I have to look after them. But that's so sort of abstract. I thought, just pack them off to school. Nothing to do with me. But then you meet them and they're actual real people. I can see so much of myself in them—in both of them. Rich is stubborn and argumentative and Jade is angry and unhelpful. But I can't blame them for being like me, can I?"

"Don't sweat it, John," Phillips said quietly. "It's a shock. You'll get over it."

"Get over it?" He sounded surprised. "I don't want to get over it. I don't want to change anything. I just want to be a good father—and I don't know how."

Ardman clicked off the MP3 player. He looked up at Rich, but he seemed to be looking past Rich, at someone standing with them at the table.

Rich turned to look and saw that Jade was there, the phone still pressed to her ear. Slowly, she lowered it and ended the call.

"We never realized," she said. Her voice sounded

strange, like it was being filtered through something that broke it up and then put it back together again slightly wrong. "He never said . . ."

Ardman picked up the phone from the table and handed it to Rich. "Adults often can't say what they mean or how they feel," he said quietly. "Which is really quite childish of us, don't you think?"

"You'll find him, won't you?" Rich said. "You'll get him back."

Ardman sighed. "Unfortunately, for all the reasons we spoke of earlier, my hands are rather tied. Yes, I'll do what I can. But I'm afraid it won't be much."

"But—this is our dad we're talking about," Jade insisted. "You have to help us."

"I can't be seen to act against Vishinsky. I told you that. I told you why. But I'll do everything I can. I promise."

"So Chance does care," Magda said. She smiled at Stabb. "Vishinsky will be so pleased to hear that. We can put pressure on Chance by threatening the children."

"Only if we have them to threaten," Stabb said. "Let's hope our luck holds. It was only by luck that you overheard the MI5 men at the Internet café mention the Clarendorf Hotel as a backup plan."

Ardman's voice was still coming through the tiny speaker on the table, but they paid it little attention now. The microphone had a built-in digital recorder that could later provide them with any information they missed.

"You said we needed them both." Magda pointed at the three people around the table in the bar below—Ardman, Rich and Jade. "There you are."

"Given what we've just learned, what we've heard, we may only need one of them." Stabb pulled a gun from inside his jacket. "But let's not look a gift horse in the mouth."

Magda took a small pistol from her handbag—the same one she had used to shoot the policeman. There was no need for the silencer this time; it was cumbersome and it slowed the bullet, making the weapon less effective.

"Let's do it," she said.

"Like I told you," Ardman said, "I can't get directly involved. Not until I have some proof about what Vishinsky is up to. My department does not officially exist and what we do is never acknowledged, but there are plenty of people who do know about us and would dearly love an excuse to shut us down. One wrong move and I'll never be in a position to help anyone again, including your father."

"So what can you do?" Jade demanded.

"I can put you in touch with someone who can help you." Ardman took a card from his jacket pocket and a fountain pen. He wrote on the back of the small card. "Dex Halford is an old colleague and friend of your father's. They were in the SAS together."

"The SAS?" Rich whistled, impressed. "He never mentioned that."

"They never do." Ardman handed the card to Jade.

"That's his address. Go and see him. He worked with your dad recently on something for me, something connected to the current situation. He may know things that can help. If nothing else, he's a good man to have with you in a crisis, even if—" He broke off.

"Even if what?" Rich wondered.

But Ardman was looking past them, toward the main door from the foyer. "Down!" he yelled, and launched himself at Jade and Rich.

Ardman's arms wrapped around Jade and dragged her into the chair where Rich was sitting—a high-backed, solid leather chair. She gave a yelp of surprise and pain. But it was drowned out by the sounds of the bullets that ripped up the carpet close to where she had been standing, and thudded into Ardman's chair, knocking it over.

The bartender had disappeared down behind the bar. Ardman struggled to pull something from his pocket. A pistol. He leaned out around the back of the chair for just long enough to fire two shots in rapid succession.

"Woman with long black hair," he said quickly as he ducked back into cover.

"That's her, Magda," Jade said, breathless. She was crushed between Rich and Ardman. More shots. They all felt the chair move, but the heavy upholstery seemed to have stopped the bullets. For the moment.

Ardman leaned out and fired twice more. "There's a man too. I'll cover you—get out quick."

Jade risked a quick look around the other side of the

chair and saw Magda aiming a pistol back at her. The man was behind her, the other side of the door, his face hidden in shadows. But there was no way past them and no other doors out of the bar.

"Get out?" Jade gasped. "How? Where? We're trapped!"

The chair shifted again as more bullets hit it. For the moment, Ardman's return fire was stopping the attackers from coming any closer. But Rich guessed it would not be long before Ardman ran out of bullets.

"Come on!" he yelled to Jade, struggling past her and out of the deep chair. He grabbed her hand. "Cover us now!" he told Ardman.

The man nodded. "Go!" As he spoke, Ardman launched himself out of the chair and rolled across the room. Bullets kicked up at the carpet around him as he dived for another chair.

And while Magda and her accomplice were shooting at Ardman, Rich dragged Jade to her feet and they ran—not toward the door, but away from it.

Rich had considered there must be a way out behind the bar, but it was too far away, and it might just lead into a room beyond with no other way in or out. So he was running head down as fast as he could for the nearest window.

"Oh, no!" Jade gasped. Rich felt her tug at his hand but he did not let go. He leaped, Jade close behind him, his shoulder down, crashing into the window, smashing his way through.

Arms up to cover their faces from flying debris, they exploded out of the hotel in a cloud of broken glass and fractured timber. They fell, rolled, and were back on their feet.

"Thanks for that," Jade said, shaking slivers of glass from her hair.

"Don't just stand there," Rich told her. "Come on!" He could hear sirens as they ran for the cover of the next street. Gunshots echoed behind them as someone fired.

Moments later, an unmarked car screeched to a halt outside the hotel, two police cars close behind it. By then, Rich and Jade were long gone.

Magda rushed upstairs, grabbed the digital recorder from the front of the gallery and slipped it into her handbag before leaving with Stabb through the door at the back.

Goddard was out of the car and through the lobby in a blur. Gun in hand, he raced into the bar. There was no sign of whoever had staged the attack, but it was apparent there had been a gun battle. He looked up to the gallery as the door swung shut, then ordered his men to spread out and search the hotel and surrounding area.

He ran to Ardman, who lay sprawled across a leather armchair. A ragged red line cut across Ardman's forehead, and blood was soaking through his jacket from a shoulder wound. Goddard yelled for the paramedics.

Ardman's eyelids flickered. "Did . . . ," he croaked. "Did they get away?"

"Clean away," Goddard told him. "I'm sorry."

Ardman clutched at Goddard's arm, shaking his head painfully. "No, the children—did they . . . ?"

"They're not here," Goddard said. "Maybe they were lucky. You did your best, sir."

"Gone to . . ." He was losing consciousness now as he tried to speak. "They've gone to . . . Gave them address . . . Gone to . . ." His voice faded.

"Where? Where have they gone? Where did you send them?" Goddard asked, aware of the two paramedics now waiting impatiently beside him.

But it was too late, Ardman was out cold. Goddard moved to let the paramedics push past. One of them quickly took Ardman's pulse.

"He's lost blood, had a nasty blow to the head," one of the paramedics said, after a brief examination. "He should be okay, but he could be out for hours."

"Hours?" Goddard asked them.

The second paramedic had lifted Ardman's eyelid and was shining a flashlight into the eye beneath.

"That might be a bit optimistic," he said. "I reckon this guy'll be out for a few days."

18

They took the Tube right to the end of the line, anxious to get as far away as possible. Then they managed to find a taxi. Rich had stopped to buy an A to Z like the one they had consulted before. Dex Halford's address was right at the edge of the area it covered. The taxi dropped them outside a farm gate, and Jade paid with almost all the rest of their money. They walked for a while, in a daze, their only thought to keep moving.

"If he doesn't help," Jade said at last, "then we'll be walking back."

"If he doesn't help, that may be the least of our problems," Rich replied.

Through the gate there was a long narrow track that led to the farmhouse where Halford apparently lived. They passed several outbuildings on the way—barns and sheds. But there was no sign of farming apart from the rough tracks. One of the barns was full of old cars, all clean and polished.

"Maybe he collects them and does them up," Rich suggested.

They turned a corner and saw that there were more cars left on the verge by the side of the track. Some were mere shells, with no wheels even. Others looked like they'd just been parked. The track led into a large farmyard and there were yet more cars parked here. In the middle of the yard was a Range Rover, and Rich could see the keys dangling in the ignition—maybe this was the vehicle Halford actually used for day-to-day driving.

"There are even cars in that barn," Jade said, pointing to a large shed. "Looks like he's repairing them."

Rich could see a ramp over a pit, with an old MG up on it so the underside could be worked on. Several others were parked around it, a Mini jacked up, an old Triumph Herald on bricks.

The track led through the farmyard and then up to a house a short distance away. The contrast was striking. Unlike the dilapidated barns and outbuildings, the farmhouse looked like it had been recently renovated and painted.

Attached to the stone building was an enormous conservatory. As they approached, Rich could see that it was a large covered swimming pool. There were plastic chairs and loungers arranged around the edge, and at the side was an area with weight machines and other gym equipment.

"Looks like he does okay out of old cars," Jade said.

"Perhaps he'll give us a lift back in one then," Rich said.

They decided to work it the same way as with Ardman, though this time Jade insisted she should be the one to go in.

"We don't know anything about this man," Rich pointed out. "How he'll react or anything. We don't really know if we can trust Ardman."

"He hasn't actually tried to kill us so far," Jade said. "That's a pretty good start."

"Yeah, but even so . . ."

"That's why only one of us goes in. It pays to be cautious." Jade took out her phone. "Same as before, only I'll call you, since your phone's almost out of time. If I keep the phone in my pocket, you'll hear everything."

"That may not be good enough." A thought occurred to Rich. "Tell him you want to sit by the pool. At least I'll be able to see you then as well."

"Oh, right. Shall I tell him I want pizza and ice cream too?"

"Think he'll do that?" Rich asked hopefully.

Jade just glared.

. . .

Dex Halford sounded pleasant, if a little bewildered, when Jade introduced herself and asked if she could come in. Halford seemed unwilling to let Jade into the house, and watching from across the yard, Rich could see the man gesturing for her to go away. It was weird—his voice was calm and reasonable, but he was trying to shoo Jade away at the same time. Almost like he knew that someone was listening in on the conversation and didn't want to upset them.

But eventually, he let Jade inside, and Rich found himself a good spot at the edge of the farmyard from where he could see into the large conservatory. He heard Jade asking if they could sit by the pool.

"I just love to sit by the poolside," she said.

"Don't overdo it," Rich muttered. He saw Jade walk into the pool room, followed by a tall man who must have been Halford. He was about the same age as their father, but he walked slowly, with the help of a stick. When he sat down on one of the plastic chairs, he stuck one leg out straight in front of him as if he had trouble bending it.

"Didn't know John Chance had kids," Halford was saying. His voice was faint but audible through the phone that Rich had jammed hard against his ear.

Halford listened while Jade gave a very brief explanation. She mentioned Rich but gave no indication he was with her or even nearby.

"So, can you help?" she asked, leaning forward from her own chair so she was close to Halford.

Rich saw the man lean forward as well. He looked to be very close to Jade now, so close that even though he seemed to be talking very quietly, his voice came clearly through the phone.

"I don't know why you came to me. It really wasn't a good move. Not a good move at all. You have no idea how much danger you are in right now."

Rich saw his sister lean back in surprise. Halford stood up, looking down at her. He suddenly looked very threatening indeed, and Rich strained to hear what the man was saying.

But all he could hear was a high-pitched whine. He checked the phone display—CALL TERMINATED. Either Jade was out of credit too or her battery had died. Typical.

Halford was leaning over Jade now and Rich could just about make out his sister's face—a mixture of anxiety and fear as she looked past Halford, down toward where Rich was hiding. But what could he do? How could he possibly help? He looked around in despair for something—any-thing—that might be of use . . .

The image through the telescopic sights of the sniper rifle was crystal clear. Magda watched as Halford leaned over Jade, talking to her urgently. Magda could not hear what Halford was saying, but then, she didn't need to. That was not her job. She was to watch and wait for the signal—if it came.

Once they had Halford's name from the digital recording made at the hotel it had been easy enough to trace him. And Magda had been waiting, watching the house through the sniper sight, until the two children arrived.

"You shouldn't have come here," Halford hissed at Jade. His face was down low, close to hers as he leaned over her menacingly. But Jade wasn't listening, wasn't even looking at him. She was staring in disbelief through the glass wall of the pool room.

The Range Rover roared up the track, bouncing along the uneven surface, lurching toward them. It didn't turn where the track bent away to the front of the farmhouse. It just kept coming in a straight line—right at the pool room. And now Jade could clearly see Rich hunched down over the steering wheel, face set in a determined stare as the Range Rover picked up speed.

The sound of the straining engine reached Halford and he turned to see what it was. He was just in time to witness the Range Rover connecting with the glass wall. Just in time to see it explode into the pool room. Just in time to dive out of the way.

Jade was up and running as the Range Rover slewed sideways in a mass of broken glass and metal. It skidded through ninety degrees before its tires found their grip on the slippery tiled floor. Then it shot forward, over the edge of the pool.

Water splashed across the room, drenching Jade.

Through it she could see the Range Rover sinking into the pool—and Rich heaving himself up onto the poolside close by. He ran toward her, slipping and sliding in his haste.

"Are you all right?" he asked as he reached her.

"You idiot," she told him. "You might have drowned!"

"That wasn't the plan," Rich admitted.

He was interrupted by the sound of laughter from nearby. Halford struggled to his feet, leaning heavily on his walking stick. He looked from the Range Rover, which was submerged in the pool, to Rich and Jade, then at the shattered side of the room. And he continued to laugh.

"I think we should get out of here," Jade said quietly. "He's mad!"

"What did you do that for?" Halford asked between guffaws of laughter.

"I came to get Jade," Rich told him.

Halford's laughter slowly subsided. "You were watching," he realized. "You thought I was threatening your sister and you came to the rescue?" Rich nodded dumbly. "By driving into my swimming pool—through the wall?"

"Well, yes."

Halford took a step toward them and raised his stick—pointing it at Rich. "Two things," he announced. "First, I wasn't threatening her; I mean her no harm at all. And I'm sorry if it seemed otherwise."

"And the second thing?" Rich said defiantly.

"The second thing is . . ." Halford paused to look again

at the wreckage around him. "You're John Chance's son, all right. Sit down and tell me what the hell's going on here. I'll do whatever I can to help."

As he was speaking, another man had walked into the pool room. He picked his way through the broken glass and bent metal from the huge windows to join them.

"I'm not as agile as I used to be," Halford said, slapping the top of his bad leg with his free hand. "Not since this. That's why I was invalided out of the army." He glanced at the newcomer before going on. "But I was lucky to be alive. Got your dad to thank for that. He dragged me out of a firefight in Afghanistan, long before we were supposed to be there. Carried me seven miles through enemy territory to get me to a safe evacuation point. I'm lucky it was just the leg."

"And who is this?" Jade asked, nodding at the man who had just arrived and who was now sitting in one of the plastic chairs listening with interest to the conversation.

"My name is Smith," he said. There was a trace of an Irish accent in his voice. "I'm a friend of Mr. Halford's and I think I may be able to help you."

"Yes," Halford said. "It's lucky that Mr. Smith arrived here just before you did." He looked at Jade, his expression solemn. "Remember what I told you just now," he said. "Mr. Smith is the man I was telling you about. Who can help."

Jade frowned, not sure what Halford meant—he hadn't said anything about a friend who could help. He'd been telling her to get out of here—up until Rich crashed the party. Literally.

From his chair nearby, Mr. Smith smiled back at Jade. He was a short man, with narrow angular features. Perhaps he too had been a soldier, wounded in action, because Jade could see a scar on his cheek—a circular shape with lines splaying out from it, like a pale spider.

19

"Let me get that drink I promised you," Halford said.

Jade didn't remember him offering a drink, but then, she had been rather distracted by Rich's arrival. And now he came to mention it, she was thirsty.

"Can I get you anything?" Halford was asking Rich. "Or you, Mr. Smith?"

While Halford disappeared into the house, Mr. Smith asked Jade and Rich to tell him their story. He listened attentively as they went through the events of the last couple of days. It didn't seem to surprise him that they were sitting beside a swimming pool with a Range Rover crashed into it, looking out over a farmyard through a hole torn in the wall . . .

Halford was soon back. Smith had declined a drink, but Rich, like Jade, had taken up the offer of lemonade. "Drink it up quick," he said. "Before the ice melts."

As soon as she took the drink, Jade could see there was something wrong. She glanced up at Halford. It looked like a fly or a bit of dirt was in her glass. But now she could see that Rich was looking curiously into his own glass. His eyes met Jade's as he looked up, widened as if he was trying to tell her something.

So Jade said nothing and looked back at her lemonade. The black shape she had thought was something floating in the liquid was actually writing—black felt-tip marker writing on the side of one of the ice cubes. It was smudging as the ice melted, and she was looking at it through the ice, so it was back to front and inside out. She prodded at the ice cube with her finger, turning it over. She licked her finger as if she was merely playing with the ice.

"So that's about it really," Rich was saying. He suddenly sounded cautious.

Looking at the melting ice, Jade could guess why. Across it, but rapidly vanishing now, in small block capital letters, Halford had written: DANGER—GET OUT.

"And you say you know nothing about this fuel sample your father is supposed to have taken?" Smith asked.

"Nothing at all," Jade said. She set down her drink on

the floor by her chair and stood up, grabbing her backpack. "Actually, I'm dying for the bathroom. Feel like I haven't been for days."

"Me too, now you mention it," Rich said, also standing. "Can you show us where it is?" he asked Halford.

Halford's mouth twitched into the vaguest hint of a smile. "Of course. Just through here. I'll show you."

But Mr. Smith was on his feet. "I don't think so," he said. "Nobody leaves."

"Or what?" Rich said.

By way of reply, the man pointed to the lemonade that Rich had just put down on a low plastic table close to where he had been sitting. A moment later, the glass exploded.

"Or that'll be your head," Smith said.

Jade felt suddenly as cold as the ice in her own drink. Rich had gone pale. Halford looked angry more than frightened. His knuckles were white as he gripped the handle of his walking stick.

"Who are you?" Jade gasped.

"His name is Stabb," Halford said. "I'm sorry, he arrived just before you did. I tried to warn you. There's a woman with a sniper rifle out there keeping watch on us." He pointed to a small raised area with trees and scrub on it close to the farmyard outside. Then he regarded the remains of Rich's glass. "Looks like she knows her stuff."

"Magda is very good," Stabb said. "But then, you already know that, don't you," he told Rich and Jade.

"And what happens now?" Rich asked. "We already told you, we don't know anything about this fuel sample."

"So you did. But your father—he knows. And now we have you, we can persuade him to tell us all about it." He smiled. "We're going on a little journey. In a plane. It's waiting at an airfield just a few miles from here. How exciting for you."

"Not sure I like the sound of that," Jade told him. "What about you, Rich?"

Rich shook his head.

"I only need one of you alive to put pressure on Chance," Stabb said. "So be careful."

But Jade wasn't listening. She was watching Halford as the man moved slowly and quietly across to one of the chairs beside the pool. He now had Stabb between himself and the direction the shot had come from—where he had pointed when he told them Magda was out there with a gun. Jade wasn't sure what—if anything—Halford was planning to do. But she tensed, bracing herself for anything.

She did not have long to wait. Halford leaned heavily on the back of the plastic chair, as if taking the weight off his bad leg. Then in a blur of rapid movement, he grabbed the back of the chair and flung it straight at Stabb.

The small man had not been expecting it, and the chair caught his legs, knocking them from under him. At the same moment, Halford dived to one side and yelled, "Get out—get out now! Run!"

Jade didn't need telling again. Rich was also prepared and was right beside her as she ran. They headed for the door into the main house rather than the broken window— that would put them right in Magda's sights. Glancing back, Jade saw Stabb struggling to his feet, pulling a pistol from the small of his back, charging after them.

She slammed the door shut, but there was no bolt or key. Rich was already racing down the narrow corridor on the other side. He reached the end and turned to the right—away from the front door. Jade ran after him. He was right, the front door would be in plain view of Magda's gun. But could they find another way out?

They dashed through a living room, then a kitchen— suddenly the back door was right ahead.

Rich ripped it open and charged through. Jade was close behind him. A gunshot—splinters of wood flew from the door frame and scraped past Jade's face, stinging her cheek. Then she was outside, still running.

She almost cannoned into Rich as he skidded to a halt in front of her.

And in front of him, rifle aimed right at them, was Magda. Her long black hair was blowing around her face in the breeze. Through it, Jade could see the woman's cruel smile.

The two of them were bundled into the back of a car. Magda sat in the front passenger seat. She had exchanged her rifle for a pistol and aimed it at them the whole time while they waited for Stabb to return from Halford's house.

He seemed to be a long time, but eventually he returned and got in the driver's seat. He started the engine.

"All dealt with?" Magda asked.

"Good enough for now," Stabb said, though he didn't sound happy.

"You killed him?" Jade accused.

"I didn't find him," Stabb said. "I would have killed him if I had. But he knows the house and the area. It's not worth spending forever looking just for the satisfaction of putting a bullet in an ex-Brit soldier with a gammy leg." He turned the car in a wide arc and headed down the track away from the farm. "But you're an easy target, so just keep quiet. Like I told you, I don't need you both. Either one will do."

"And you don't have to be in perfect health," Magda added. "Remember that."

Jade shuddered and fumbled for Rich's hand. They sat in silence for the rest of the short journey.

The airfield was indeed only a few miles away. It was barely more than a big field, with a hut at one end and a single concrete runway. There were several light aircraft arranged around the edge of the field. A larger, newer and more impressive executive jet was waiting on the runway. Jade could hear the engines already running as they drove right up to it.

"Just leaving the car here?" Rich asked as they were told to get out.

"Why not?" Magda said. "It isn't ours."

"It'll be taken care of," Stabb said. He turned to speak to the uniformed steward who was coming down the steps from the plane's door. "You're ready to go—that's very impressive."

"The man from the control hut came over to tell us you were on your way," the steward said in accented English. "I assumed you called ahead."

Stabb shook his head. "No."

"They must have seen the car as we approached," Magda said. "We are ready to leave?"

The steward nodded. "All ready."

Jade and Rich were sent up the steps and into the plane at gunpoint. Once inside, the steward produced several lengths of stout cord. "Hands together, please," he said. Rich and Jade put their hands out in front of them.

"Keep your wrists apart if you can," Rich whispered as the steward selected one of the cords. "And tense your muscles as much as possible."

Jade wasn't sure what he was getting at, but she tried. The cords bit into her wrists as the steward pulled them tight. As soon as he had tied their wrists, he led them to seats at the front of the plane. There was plenty of legroom before the bulkhead in front of them—and also plenty of room for the steward to kneel down and tie their ankles together. When he was done, he tossed Jade's backpack onto the spare seat beside her. She guessed he'd already been through the contents—probably taken her phone.

"Never did get to the bathroom," Jade said. "Can't even cross my legs now."

"Wonder where we're going," Rich said. But they both had a pretty good idea of the destination.

The sound of the engines deepened and the plane hurtled down the runway.

Once they were in the air, Stabb came to see them. "You can save yourselves a lot of unpleasantness, you know," he said. "You and your dad."

"Really?" Rich said. "How's that then?" He was feeling queasy and it wasn't that he got airsick. He was afraid of what might happen to him, and even more terrified about what they'd do to Jade.

"Just tell me where it is," Stabb said.

"This fuel sample?" Jade said. "We don't know. We told you, we don't know."

"Why's it so important anyway?" Rich demanded. "What is it? If you told us, maybe we could work out where Dad might have hidden it."

Stabb nodded. "Maybe. It is the only surviving sample of a very special fuel developed in Vishinsky's London laboratory. Well," he said, "the fuel itself is not important. It's what is in it that matters."

"And why do you need it?" Jade wanted to know.

"Because we don't have the formula. We need the sample to reverse engineer so we can manufacture the substance in bulk." He leaned forward and stared first at Jade, then at Rich. "So, where is it?"

"I don't know," Jade said.

"But we'll think about it," Rich added hurriedly. "See if we can work out where Dad might have put it."

"You do that," Stabb said. "You've got until we land. That's about another three hours."

"Three hours," Jade said when Stabb was gone. "That's ages."

"Good," Rich replied. "Because that's how long we have to get these ropes off. I've been trying, but he tied me up too tight. You have to compress your muscles now and try to wriggle your hand out. Push your thumb into the middle of your palm so your hand is smaller."

Jade was trying. "Where did you learn escapology then, Houdini?"

"Read how to do it in a book."

"Very helpful."

"If you can get free it will be."

"Why me?" Jade hissed.

"Because he won't have tied you up so tight," Rich told her. He grinned. "Because you're a girl, so he wouldn't want to hurt you."

"More likely my muscles are better trained than yours and my wrists are slimmer," she told him.

"You wish." Rich was heartened to see that Jade managed a weak smile at his comment.

"You know," Jade said, "boarding school might not be so bad after all."

Rich nodded. "Can't be much worse than real life," he agreed.

An hour later, Jade could barely feel her hands, and her wrists were red, raw from rubbing against the cords. Rich's own wrists were still bound tight, but Jade looked like she was making progress—she could slide one of her hands almost halfway out of the loop of cord now.

"You're doing well," he told her quietly. "You're getting there."

"Thanks," she said. "Neat trick with the Range Rover, by the way."

"Just fancied a drive. That's all."

"Didn't know you could drive," Jade said.

"Neither did I," Rich told her.

Jade smiled at him. "Mum would have been proud."

"Of you too," Rich said. For a moment the twins looked at each other. Neither of them needed to say anything else.

It took Jade over another hour, but finally she got her hand free.

"Well done," Rich said. "That's great. Get your legs free, then you can try to untie me."

"I'll untie you first," Jade said.

But Rich shook his head. "No, we're starting to descend, can't you tell?"

"So?"

"So it won't help if we just have our hands free. Get your legs free, so you can make a run for it if you get the chance. Then untie me."

"Okay."

Jade set to work on her legs, leaning down and pretending to be slumped forward asleep while reaching down to fumble with the knots at her ankles. Rich looked out of the window, trying to take in as much detail as possible.

The plane was emerging from the low clouds as it came down. Below them was an airfield. It looked like a military base, with low barracks buildings and soldiers drilling to the side of the runways. There was a barbed wire perimeter, with a single main gate guarded by soldiers.

As the pilot lined the plane up with the runway, Rich noticed a large black limousine waiting at the other end, along with several camouflage-green trucks and jeeps. And a large tank, its gun aimed back along the runway.

"Done it!" Jade whispered, sitting back up.

"Look," Rich said, nodding at the window. Jade leaned across to see.

"Make sure your seat belts are fastened," Stabb said, appearing in the aisle beside them. He sat down on the other side of the aisle. "Impressive display, don't you think? Quite a welcome."

"Yes," Rich said. He felt numb. Maybe Jade had managed to get free, but they were about to land in the middle of an army base. "Vishinksy must be a powerful guy."

Stabb fastened his seat belt. "Money can buy anything,"

he said. "Even the help of the local armed forces. Welcome to Krejikistan."

Rich looked at Jade. He tried to smile, to offer some encouragement. But he couldn't do it. "Sorry," he mouthed.

"It's okay," she murmured back. But they both knew that it wasn't.

They had given Chance a thin mattress that lay on the hard concrete floor. The room was small and plain and square, with a bucket in the corner. No windows and only one door.

He had been in similar situations over the years. Each time he wondered if he would ever leave the room they had shut him in. Chance knew that a large part of the trick of surviving was staying optimistic—never giving up. The more alert and upbeat you were, the better your chances of making the most of any opportunity to escape.

And now there was one thing that kept him going above all.

Alone in a cell in the middle of Krejikistan, Chance was taking courage from the fact that his children were safely in London, thousands of miles away.

20

The plane was slowing as it taxied the last hundred yards along the runway to the waiting convoy of vehicles. Through the window, Jade could see a set of steps on wheels standing ready at one side of the runway just in front of the black limousine.

Under cover of leaning to see out of the window, and while Stabb, Magda and everyone else were waiting for the plane to stop, Jade tried to untie Rich's hands. But the knots were too tight and her numb fingers were making no headway.

"Leave me," Rich whispered.

"No way."

"Just escape while you can. At least with one of us free there's some hope." He tried to sound upbeat.

"I can't just leave you!" Jade insisted. Her fair hair fell forward, hiding her pained expression.

"You can. You must. Please, it's the only hope for both of us. Once this plane stops, we haven't a chance."

Jade's mouth dropped open. "You want me to get out before it stops?!"

"You'll be okay. I've—"

"I know," she interrupted, "you've read about it in a book or somewhere. Great. Thanks. You're crazy, you know that, right?"

"I'm not the one who has to jump out of a moving plane," Rich pointed out.

The plane was slowing. It was now or never. Jade took a deep breath. Then she leaped to her feet and ran.

The plane was still moving. Stabb saw her and tugged at his seat belt. Farther down the aisle, Magda was also trying to get up. But Jade was already at the door at the front of the cabin.

There was a long lever, horizontal across the door with a large painted red arrow showing which way it turned in an emergency.

Well, if this wasn't an emergency, then nothing was, Jade thought as she wrenched the lever around.

• • •

Rich watched in horror as Stabb brought out his gun. Jade was still at the door. Stabb was taking aim, about to shoot her down.

With his hands and legs tied together, Rich stood up, almost overbalancing. He managed to turn his sideways momentum into a jump—launching himself off his tied-together feet across the aisle.

He crashed into Stabb, sending the man sprawling over the seats. The gun skidded out of his grasp.

With a hydraulic hiss the door swung open. The hiss became an explosion of sound—the wind whipped past the jet, which was still traveling at twenty miles an hour. There was a rush of compressed air as the inflatable slide billowed out from beneath the door. Without waiting for it to finish, without wondering whether her weight would be enough to drag the slide down to the ground, Jade jumped.

She hit the chute and bounced, then slid toward the runway that was hurtling past. Her foot dug into the plastic, caught, was free again—and now she tumbled.

Luckily, she was rolling with the fall. She reached out for the runway as it skimmed past, and tumbled out across it, onto the grass on the other side. Her ankles were numb from where the ropes had been tied so tight. Her foot was protesting where it had snagged. Her legs felt like jelly. But she was on her feet and running as fast as she could for the nearest building—a long, low storage hangar.

• • •

As soon as the plane had stopped, Stabb shoved Rich out of the door. Without the full use of hands or legs, Rich rolled and tumbled down the inflated slide and bumped painfully onto the runway at the bottom.

Magda was close behind him, then Stabb. Immediately, Stabb was yelling at the soldiers grouped around the waiting vehicles. He waved them toward a nearby hangar and Rich guessed that was where Jade had been heading. There was no sign of her now. He just hoped she had managed to get away.

A soldier yanked Rich to his feet and pushed him toward the black limo. With his ankles tied, Rich immediately fell over again, but he managed to get his hands out to stop himself getting hurt in the fall.

Magda leaned over him, brandishing a knife. It was a vicious-looking weapon with a blade that was serrated on one side. Rich tried to shuffle away from her as the knife came closer to his face. The woman smiled and reached down to cut through the cords binding his ankles.

"Did you think I was going to cut you?" she said, amused. "Well, maybe I will. Later." She sliced through the cords around his wrists, then stood up and walked to the limousine. "Bring him," she called to the soldiers standing over Rich.

He was bundled into the limo. Magda was sitting in the middle of the wide bench seat. On the other side of her was a man. Rich recognized him at once from the pictures he and Jade had seen on the KOS Web site at the Internet café—Viktor Vishinsky.

It was an optical illusion. Jade hadn't intended it to work that way, but she realized as soon as the soldiers raced into the hangar what had happened. She had almost—so nearly—run into the hangar. But at the last moment it occurred to her that if she did, there might be no way out. She could be trapped.

And that would indeed have been the case, judging by the amusement and confidence of the soldiers who soon arrived and ran into the hangar after her, or so they thought. Jade had run past the doors, down the side of the hangar. But anyone watching from a distance, expecting her to go inside, would have assumed that was what she'd done as she disappeared from sight, level with the dark opening of the doorway.

Her problem now was what to do next—there was nowhere else to go. There were plenty of other buildings on the air base, but they were all a long way away. She'd be spotted well before she got to any of them. And it wouldn't take long for the soldiers to finish searching the hangar and conclude either that she'd escaped somehow or that she had never gone inside.

"Think, think . . . ," Jade urged herself. She tried to decide what Rich would do. He'd probably tell her to do something stupid, or make some comment that sounded really useful but was no help at all. Like: "Hide in the last place they'd ever think to look." Right—big help. But where was the last place they'd ever think to look?

Jade was peering around the side of the hangar, desperately searching for some hiding place. And then she saw it—not fifty yards away. With luck she could get there without being spotted. And yes, it had to be the last place anyone would think to look for her.

The plane she'd just escaped from.

It was still on the runway, the inflated chute hanging from its side. There was a large cargo bay door open at the back now, forming a ramp sloping down to the runway. If she could get to that before the soldiers came out of the hangar . . .

The limousine and some of the other vehicles in the convoy were already pulling away. The plane had turned slightly since it arrived, to allow for easier unloading. But now the bags and crates had been removed, and it was between Jade and the vehicles, shielding her from sight. If she was lucky.

Not that she had much choice, she decided. She took a deep breath, quickly checked that the way was clear and there was no one coming out of the hangar. Then she ran.

She was out of breath, gasping, as she charged up the ramp into the cargo bay. She looked around, checking there was no one else there. But the place seemed deserted. It was cramped and she had to duck her head as she made her way into the gloomy space, negotiating the cargo nets that held down freight when the plane was loaded and airborne.

Luckily, there was plenty of room behind the various crates and boxes still in the hold for her to hide. Jade knelt down in the shadows, behind a huge packing crate. Peering out, she had a good view out of the back of the plane and across the airfield. She could see the hangar beside which she had been hiding. There was no sign of activity—no one running after her, shouting, pointing . . .

Jade breathed a huge sigh of relief. And then a hand clamped over her mouth, pulling her backward into the darkness of the cargo hold.

Watching the soldiers through the window of the limousine, Rich hoped against hope that Jade was all right. Stabb was standing at the back with a group of uniformed troops, shouting at them.

"Your sister is causing Mr. Stabb some trouble," Vishinsky said to Rich. He seemed amused rather than angry. He leaned forward and spoke to the driver in, Rich assumed, Russian.

The limo pulled away slowly, turning in a wide circle. It slowed as it reached Stabb, and Vishinsky wound down his window.

"Don't waste your time. Leave it to them," he said. "They know what they are doing, and—where can she go?"

Stabb nodded and said something else to the soldiers.

But Vishinsky's window was rising and the car was moving faster now, so Rich could not hear what he was saying. He saw Stabb run over to a jeep and climb in beside the driver. Two jeeps were now following the limousine onto a service road and toward the main gate out of the air base.

"Do you know what this is?" Vishinsky asked as they headed for the main gate out of the base. He reached across Magda and handed Rich a large, plain brown envelope.

Rich opened it cautiously and found it contained three large photographs. They were black-and-white, grainy and indistinct. He wasn't even sure at first which way up they should be.

"Yes, they are not very good, I'm afraid," Vishinsky said. "Blowups from a security camera. I am assured they have been enhanced as much as is possible. More than is possible, if my experts are to be believed."

He reached over again and tapped at something in the middle of the top picture. "This—what is it?"

Rich had just about managed to work out that he was looking at a close-up shot of a hand. The hand was holding something—the thing that Vishinsky had pointed to. The other photos were almost identical—the hand moving only slightly between the frames.

"No," Rich said. "No, sorry, I don't know." He shook his head. "It's pretty small, judging by the size of the hand. And there's a picture on the thing, a pattern or outline or something. Not very clear." He put the photos back in the envelope and returned it to Vishinsky.

Rich turned to look out the window. The countryside looked bare and barren with a little grass poking through the dry ground. In the distance there were hills, which looked just as dry and dusty brown. He had been careful not to show it, but the picture had reminded Rich of something. He just couldn't remember what. Maybe nothing at all, he decided. The shape on whatever it was that the hand was holding was hardly unusual. But he couldn't help thinking he'd seen it somewhere recently—a simple outline of a heart.

Jade stopped struggling as soon as she saw who it was. Dex Halford took his hand from Jade's mouth and put his finger to his own lips to warn her to be quiet. Together, they ducked down behind the crate.

"How did you get here?" Jade whispered.

"I could ask you the same thing," Halford said quietly. "It wasn't hard to guess where they were taking you when Stabb mentioned a nearby airfield. There aren't a lot of choices. It's quicker across the back fields than by road, and your brother had at least left me a working tractor, even if my Range Rover will need towing out of the pool when I finally get home."

"You stowed away?" Jade realized. "In here?"

Halford nodded. "Told the crew they were to prepare for takeoff, which I expected they'd find out soon enough anyway. The moment they weren't looking I sneaked in while the back was open. What about you?"

Jade shrugged. "Managed to get free and jumped. Then I legged it."

"That why it was a bumpy landing?" Halford smiled. "I'm bruised all over."

"They've still got Rich," Jade said. "I couldn't get him out too."

"That's all right," Halford said, suddenly serious. "Let's go and get him back."

"And how do we do that?"

Halford peered around the crate and then got unsteadily to his feet, pushing himself up with his walking stick. "We start by stealing a jeep," he said.

Although some of the military vehicles had followed Vishinsky's car from the air base, there were still a couple of jeeps, a large truck and the tank on the runway close to the plane. Most of the soldiers had gone to help with the search for Jade—still centered on the hangar fifty yards away. It looked like it might be possible to get to a jeep, but Jade wasn't sure what they'd do then—could they even get off the base?

Halford couldn't run—the best he could manage was a fast hobble, leaning heavily on his stick as they left the plane. Things went wrong almost at once.

A soldier came around the side of the plane, heading back toward the convoy of vehicles. He almost walked into Jade and Halford as they emerged down the cargo ramp.

The speed of Halford's reaction took Jade by surprise. She hardly had time to see his arm shoot out before the soldier was lying unconscious on the ground and his rifle was somehow in Halford's hand.

But one of the soldiers by the nearest jeep had either seen or heard. He was shouting to the others, pointing. Then suddenly he was diving for cover as Halford put a bullet into the ground close to his feet.

"Pity," he said. "But maybe that was looking too easy."

The soldiers were firing back now, and Halford and Jade were forced to duck for cover of their own behind the tank. Jade hoped there was no one inside it. The hatch on the top was standing open, which was a good sign. She didn't want to think what might happen if the gun swung around to fire at them or if the huge armored vehicle started to move. She pressed herself against the cold metal as Halford leaned around to fire. He pulled back before another volley of shots pinged off the armor plating close by.

"Can't keep them pinned down for long," Halford warned. "I might be able to cover you so you can get to one of the jeeps."

"Then what?" Jade had to shout to be heard above the rattle of gunfire.

"Drive it over here and pick me up." He made it sound so easy.

"Yeah, right," Jade muttered, bracing herself to run through a hail of bullets. "Let's hope they left the keys for us." Maybe this wasn't the best time to confess she had little idea how to drive.

But as it turned out, she didn't have to. A soldier appeared from the other side of the plane, behind them—running straight at the tank. Halford hadn't seen him yet and the soldier was already bringing up his machine pistol.

Jade yelled. But her shout was lost in the rattle of machine-gun fire. Bullets kicked up earth, stitching a line across the ground close to Halford. He was turning, aiming the rifle, but too late.

The line of bullets reached Halford, drilling into his leg, cutting right through it. Jade screamed as Halford's leg was severed at the knee, coming completely away. He gave an angry shout and collapsed.

21

Halford was staring in disbelief at the ragged end of his trousers, where his knee had been. "You shot my leg off!" he shouted in disbelief.

Jade was staring in disbelief too. She was expecting blood to be pumping out, Halford to be unconscious—maybe even dead. But there was no sign of any blood, and the man seemed angry more than in pain.

The soldier who had shot Halford also looked confused. He hesitated, then brought the gun up again.

But Halford recovered first and fired a single rifle shot

from the ground. It caught the soldier in the shoulder, spinning him around and slamming him to the runway.

"Just a flesh wound," Halford assured Jade.

"He shot your leg off!" she said.

"I meant him—he's just got a flesh wound. I can manage without my leg," he assured her, heaving himself up on his stick. "God knows, I've managed without it for long enough already."

And only then did Jade realize why Halford walked with a stick and a limp. "You've got an artificial leg."

"Not anymore," he said, prodding at the detached lower leg with his walking stick. "And with it goes our chance of getting to a jeep. Too many soldiers out there now." He paused as the tank rang with the sound of bullets impacting on its armor. "They'll soon realize we're pinned down and rush us. I doubt I can hop out of here, but I'm open to any other suggestions."

Jade could think of only one possibility. Desperate, and probably stupid, and definitely dangerous, but it was all she could offer. "Can you drive a tank?" she asked.

The sergeant in charge of the soldiers with the convoy knew he had them beaten. Stabb had told him he could kill the girl if he had to, but it probably wouldn't be necessary. She and the man who had appeared from the cargo hold of the plane were pinned down behind the tank. And the soldiers that the sergeant had recalled from searching the hangar would be able to come around behind them. There was no way they could escape. He smiled confidently and gave the order into his radio for the troops to move in.

He had barely finished speaking when there was a shout from the soldier next to him and a burst of rapid fire. The sergeant looked up in time to see the hatch on top of the tank turret slam shut. He swore. It might take a while to get them out, but they were still trapped—inside the tank. Things could be worse.

Then the huge powerful engines of the tank coughed into life and things were worse. The tank was moving. Slowly, ponderously at first, but picking up speed, the tank headed right at the sergeant and his men. They fired at it, a storm of bullets rattling off the tank to no effect.

Suddenly men were running out of the way of the tank and away from the jeeps and the truck. The tank plowed into the side of the truck, ripping off its canvas cover and crunching through the back axle. The truck lurched sideways and stood at an ungainly angle as the tank passed—moving on to the jeeps behind.

One of the jeeps was shunted aside so violently, it rolled and bounced across the runway. The tank drove straight over the other one, its tracks biting into the side of the jeep as the heavy tank rose up over it, before smashing down and crushing the smaller vehicle.

The sergeant was shouting into his radio, alerting the soldiers at the main gate and giving them instructions, but he doubted anyone was listening. He could already see the guards running from their hut by the gate. Moments later, the tank drove right through it—gate, hut, fence. Planks of wood went flying. Glass exploded into fragments. Barbed wire stretched and tore. Dry earth was flying up from the tank's tracks as it rumbled across the road and onto the bare ground beyond.

The road through the wilderness swung in a long loop from the air base to the main road, so Rich found that he could see the base in the distance out of the side window of the limousine as it reached the outermost point of the curve in the road.

He was looking straight at it when the gate and the hut beside it exploded into fragments and a large battle tank smashed through. Brown dust trailed behind it like smoke as the tank set off toward the main road. But it wasn't using the looping service road that the limo and jeeps had taken. It was heading in a straight line—a far shorter distance.

Rich watched, holding his breath and trying to work out if the tank would reach the main road before they did. He didn't know who was driving the tank, but he could make a pretty good guess. "Beats a Range Rover," he murmured to himself. "Why does she always have to go one better?" He wondered how long it would be before someone else noticed . . .

The driver pulled a cell phone from his pocket. He listened for a moment, then turned to look out of his side window in surprise. The car lurched as he saw the tank heading rapidly for the road ahead of the convoy. Vishinsky and Magda, alerted by the jolt, were also staring in amazement out the window.

Rich couldn't understand any of what the driver was telling Vishinsky, but he was delighted to see that the man didn't take it like good news. The limo sped up—trying to beat the tank to the junction ahead.

It was going to be a close call. One of the two jeeps following the limo had veered off the service road and was bouncing toward the tank. The soldiers in the jeep were being thrown around as it sped over the uneven ground. The driver got in front of the tank and turned his vehicle toward it—heading straight at the tank. The other soldiers were waving at the tank to stop. Then, as the tank showed no sign of stopping, they shot at it with their rifles.

The tank didn't even slow down. Two of the soldiers in the back jumped out, rolling across the ground. At what seemed like later than the last minute, the driver tried to steer out of the tank's way. He was too late. The driver leaped after the last of his passengers, and a split second later the tank smashed into the jeep. Its hood crumpled, dragged under the tank tracks as the tank lurched upward, then slammed down and kept going.

The limo's engine roared as the driver dropped a gear in an attempt to accelerate more quickly. But he had left it too late. The tank was almost at the junction where the service road fed into a ramp on to the main highway. One of the treads stopped moving suddenly and the tank skidded around so it was pointing right at the limo and blocking the entrance to the ramp.

The driver wrenched at the wheel, and it looked like he was going to be able to steer the big car around the tank and back onto the road. Rich brought his feet up and kicked out as hard as he could. The soles of his shoes hammered into the back of the driver's seat, sending shock waves right up Rich's legs. He could feel his seat belt cutting across him.

But it had the right effect. The driver lurched forward over the wheel and the limousine smashed into the front of the tank. The hood shot up and a cloud of steam erupted from beneath. The engine stopped, leaving only the rumble of the tank's engines. The driver stayed slumped forward.

Magda was already fumbling for her gun when Rich's door was dragged open and he almost fell out.

"Jade!"

"Don't just sit there, come on!" she yelled at him, pulling him from the car.

Magda's hand came up and Rich kicked the door shut behind him. His whole body felt battered and bruised, but he wasn't about to get shot. He heard the bullet thud into the door and Vishinsky yelling in Russian. Then he was running with Jade for the tank.

He was astonished to see Halford's upper body sticking out of the hatch in the turret. Where had he come from? The man had a machine pistol and was firing at the soldiers and Mr. Stabb in the remaining jeep, keeping them pinned down. Seeing Rich with Jade, he gave a grin and changed his aim slightly.

Steam rose from the jeep's radiator and then the front tires exploded. It wasn't going to be following them any more than the wrecked limo was, Rich realized. Jade ran around to the back of the tank so they could climb up without fear of being shot at by the soldiers in the useless jeep.

They hauled themselves up to the turret just as Halford ran out of ammunition. His gun clicked uselessly and he cursed. "Hurry it up!" he shouted to Jade and Rich. They were almost there. Halford was already ducking back down inside the tank turret when a bullet hit him.

Rich saw the surprise and pain on the man's face as he was slammed back into the unforgiving metal of the hatchway. He clutched at his shoulder, and blood trickled out from between his fingers. Then he slid slowly out of sight.

"In—get in!" Jade yelled, pushing Rich after Halford through the hatch. No sooner was he inside the cramped space than Jade was after him, dragging the hatch closed behind her.

"Got to get moving," Halford gasped. His whole hand was stained red. "Jade—you know what to do?"

"I think so."

There was barely room to move inside the cabin of the

tank. Rich couldn't even stand up. It sounded like a hailstorm as bullets pinged off the tank's outer shell.

Rich watched in amazement as Jade hurried to the controls. "You can drive a tank?"

She gave him a nervous smile. "Easy enough. These two levers control the tracks—one for each side. Push both forward to go forward, or pull them back for reverse. Just one track at a time will turn, so that's how you steer. Don't worry—I've been taking lessons."

She hesitated, flexing her fingers before reaching for the two levers.

"And how do you stop?" Rich asked.

Jade looked at her brother.

"We didn't get to that bit," she replied, and smiled again.

The man wasn't really called Ralph, but that was the name Halford had listed in his cell phone. Halford's vision was blurring, so he got Rich to dial. Rich then handed him back the phone.

Jade, meanwhile, had taken the tank off the main highway at the first junction and was looking for a suitable place to try to stop. Somewhere inconspicuous but easy to describe to "Ralph." Eventually, she turned into the forecourt of a derelict gas station. The awning was still there, stained and at a drunken angle, but the pumps were gone, and the kiosk that might also have been a little shop was boarded up. There was space at the back, behind the kiosk and out of sight of the road.

She described where they were to Halford and he relayed the information in Russian to Ralph. When he had finished, he looked exhausted.

"If I lose consciousness," he said, trying to raise himself up into a sitting position, "then wait for Ralph. He isn't the most savory of characters, but he owes me a favor. He'll help."

"Who is he?" Rich wondered. "What does he do? Is he in the government or police or something?"

Halford forced a smile. "Not quite. Let's just say he's a businessman and leave it at that, shall we?"

"A businessman?" Jade said. "What sort of business?"

"Well, not really what you'd call legitimate business," Halford admitted.

"You mean he's a gangster?" Rich said.

Jade shook her head in disbelief. "Terrific. Just the sort of help we need."

"Against Vishinsky, it is," Halford told her. He sagged back, breathing deeply, eyes closed.

"Thanks for coming to get me," Rich said to his sister. "I knew you would."

"Don't take me for granted," Jade warned him.

"Well, I didn't expect you in a tank."

Ralph arrived in a large dark Mercedes. It pulled quietly onto the forecourt, headlights cutting through the night.

The back door opened and a man got out. He was short but thick-set, with a heavy brow, combed black hair and a shiny pinstripe suit.

The driver and two other men followed Ralph closely, over to where the children were waiting. They all wore pinstripe suits. They helped get Halford out of the tank and put him carefully in the back of the car.

"We shall leave your tank here," Ralph told them. He grinned, showing off a gold tooth at the front of his mouth.

"It's not really ours," Rich protested.

Ralph shrugged. "What do you say? Finder's keepers? It is yours now."

"You'll look after Halford?" Jade asked.

"A doctor is examining him in the car. He will do what he can. We can get him to a safe hospital, but it looks like it was a clean shot—the bullet went right through." He smiled again. "I have some experience of gunshot wounds."

"I bet," Jade said. "So what's your real name? It's not Ralph."

The man frowned. "Ralph? Halford said my name was Ralph?" He chuckled. "It is as good a name as any. It will do. Yes, I like it. Ralph." He clicked his fingers and one of the men in pinstripes stepped closer. Ralph talked to him rapidly in Russian and the man handed over a cell phone.

Ralph handed the phone to Rich. "Speed dial six will get through to me at once. Don't worry, the phone is untraceable."

"Is it stolen?" Rich asked.

"Acquired. We will look after Halford. Do not worry. I owe him much. He said, when he called, that you are going to rescue your father from Vishinsky."

"That's right," Jade said.

Ralph whistled. "Rather you than me. He also said that your father is a man I know as Harry." He held his hands up before either Jade or Rich could reply. "I do not need or want to know his real name. That would not help any of us, any more than my real name would help you. I only know Halford is a real name by accident. But I owe Harry as much as I owe Halford. I cannot move directly against Vishinsky, you understand."

"Why not?" Rich wanted to know.

"Politics. Economics. Boring reasons. But at the moment the state is not too hard on us, so we have an understanding. It works for us and it works for them too. But if I am seen to oppose Vishinsky, then that could change. If the criminals who run our country, our police and armed forces, have to decide who they most need—me or Vishinsky . . ." He opened his hands. "I would not bet on me coming out as favorite."

"So are you just going to abandon us here or what?" Jade asked.

"I could not do that. I said I cannot be seen to help, but I will do what I can."

"Which is what?" Rich said.

"Another car will be here soon. The driver will have

certain things for you that Mr. Halford has suggested may be useful, and the car will take you close to the main KOS pumping station. It is Vishinsky's base of operations, though he has his own castle in the foothills of the mountains to the north. But it is at the pumping station he is keeping your father."

"How do you know?" Rich asked.

"Because he bribes soldiers to take him there and to keep quiet. I bribe soldiers again to tell me everything that Vishinsky wants them to keep quiet about. Probably he bribes them a third time to let him know what they have told me, but I really can't afford to bribe them a fourth time to find out."

"And Dad's definitely there?" Jade said.

"He was taken there. He nearly escaped, which amused the soldier who told me. He has not been taken away and I have asked where he is being held—it is a big facility. If we have news, the driver will tell you when he comes. It will not be long. I did consider bribing soldiers to bring your father to me, but I am afraid there is no profit in it, and Vishinsky would not be pleased. By all the accounts I am getting, your father is very important to him."

"It's what he has that's important," Rich said.

"Or rather, what he has hidden," Jade added.

"Oh?" Ralph's eyes were shining with curiosity. But before either of them could answer he laughed. "Better you do not tell me that either. Better that I don't know."

His smile faded. "Better you get into the habit of trusting no one, however friendly they may seem. You were lucky to find Halford—he is a rare breed. But in this world you have fallen into, this dark and dangerous world, no one is what they seem and no one has any interest in anything other than themselves."

"Including you?" Rich asked.

Ralph smiled again. "Especially me. I have been in this business a long time now, and you know what I have learned?"

"What?" Jade prompted.

"Survival—that is all there is. The money is easy. The money is cheap. The money doesn't matter." He patted Jade on the shoulder. "Look after yourselves. Both of you." He reached out to shake hands with Rich. "I have to leave now."

"Can we see Halford?" Jade asked. "Before you go?"

Halford was conscious, but obviously woozy from an injection to ease the pain. He lay along the backseat, his shoulder bandaged, blood already seeping through.

"We take him to a hospital. Do good job there," the doctor assured them. "He be all right. Tough as old shoes, this one."

"Just leave me," Halford whispered. He struggled to sit up. "Thanks, but leave me. I'll be fine with Ralph. And I'll put in a call to Ardman. Vishinsky won't be looking for me anyway. You find your dad."

"You're a grown-up," Jade told him. "You're supposed to tell us not to be so stupid, not to go it alone, not to do anything dangerous but to wait for proper help and the professionals."

"And would you listen?" Halford asked.

"Course not," Rich told him.

"Didn't reckon you would, either of you," Halford said. His speech was slurring. "I'll be fine," he said slowly and weakly. "I can tell who your father is, all right." The door closed and the car turned out onto the road.

"He'll be okay," Rich told Jade. He hoped that just saying it would help make it true.

"I know," she said. "And we have to find Dad."

Another car was turning in. It parked under the broken awning and flashed its lights at them.

"Let's find Dad then," Rich said, walking with Jade to the car. "At least we have the element of surprise. They might be looking for us, but they won't expect us to come after them."

"We'll find them," Stabb promised. "I think I winged the man Halford."

"They can hardly hide a tank," Magda agreed. "It won't take long."

"Don't even bother," Vishinsky said. "Don't waste your time." They were all three sitting in the back of a replacement limousine, heading through the evening to the main KOS installation. The first limousine was a write-off, and they had left the driver still out cold over the wheel. Stabb's jeep had to be towed off for a new engine and tires.

"What do you mean?" Magda asked.

"They think they are so clever," Vishinsky said. "But we have something they want very badly."

"Chance," Stabb said, amused. "They'll try to find Chance."

"And I have made sure that it is well known where we are holding him. They will come to the main plant," Vishinsky agreed. "And when they do, we shall be waiting for them."

22

On the journey across town, Rich and Jade went through the stuff in the backpack and carryall that the driver had brought. He had also given them bulky, padded coats, which they put on to ward off the increasing cold of the night.

Some of the other stuff was obviously useful—like wire cutters, and a map of the KOS installation with security cameras marked and a large red arrow pointing at one small building in the middle where Chance was being held.

Some of the things were probably useful, but Rich and

Jade agreed they would not take them—including hand-guns. Other stuff they had no idea what it was—like metal canisters with levers held by pins attached. They might be grenades or they might be fizzy drinks, Rich and Jade couldn't tell—and didn't try to open them to find out. There was also a small black box with a switch on it next to a small blank display screen. Rich was careful not to touch the switch. The box, and anything else he wasn't sure about, Rich stuffed back into the backpack.

"Dad'll probably know what to do with it," he said.

"You going to take him a gun as well?"

Rich considered this. "I'd rather not."

"Good." She rummaged through the small backpack she had managed to keep with her throughout and pulled out a packet of cigarettes. "His cell's gone, but I've still got these."

Rich took the packet and opened it. There were six cigarettes left, and Chance's lighter was pushed inside the packet too. He closed it and handed it back to Jade. "You took them. You should give them back."

"Okay."

The driver seemed to speak no English. He dropped them beside a narrow service road apparently in the middle of nowhere. But in the distance, they could see the huge KOS facility outlined in black against the deep gray of the night sky.

Before leaving them, the driver took the map from Rich,

opened it on the hood of the car and jabbed a finger at a point on the edge of the installation.

"Good place to break in?" Rich said. "Thanks."

The driver indicated another point on the perimeter. He gave an exaggerated shrug. Evidently, each place was as good—or bad—as the first.

"So where are we now?" Jade asked. She pointed down at the ground. "Here. Where?" She pointed at the edge of the map, outside the installation and mimicked the driver's exaggerated shrug.

He nodded to show he understood and indicated a point on a narrow road leading past the back of the complex.

Jade stared. "But that's miles away."

"I thought you liked exercise," Rich said. "And anyway—it's a nice night for a walk."

It seemed to take forever to get across the undulating barren landscape to the KOS installation. As they approached they could hear clanking and hissing and the flare of burning oil. They could see plumes of fire and smoke from various points of the facility. And they could taste the fuel in the air, acrid and oily.

"You realize we'll never get past all those cameras," Rich said. "Not without some massive distraction."

"I do," Jade said. "And I've been thinking about that."

"Got a plan?"

"Got an idea. You help me make it into a plan."

Rich listened. He liked the idea, but he didn't like what

it meant for Jade. They spent the rest of the journey to the facility talking about how to make it work.

Two figures approached the perimeter fence, silhouetted in black against the gray of the outer buildings and the puddles of security lighting. They were both the same height, and both were padded out in the bulky coats the driver had given them. Even in the glow of the security lights as they reached the fence, they were barely indistinguishable with their similar features and identical expressions—grim and determined. Only the longer hair of one of them, hanging past her shoulders, marked Jade as different from her brother.

"Good luck," Rich said quietly.

"You too."

Jade hugged her brother tightly for a moment. "Right, me first with the wire cutters," she said. "Then I'll give you ten minutes. That enough?"

Rich nodded. "See you soon."

Vishinsky was drinking vodka in the boardroom right in the heart of the office section of the KOS facility. A large, polished antique wooden table dominated the room, and Vishinsky was sitting at the head of it. He was alone. Along one side of the room was a set of cupboards and filing cabinets. On top of this was a tray of decanters and glasses. Vishinsky got up and went to refill his shot glass. He sniffed appreciatively at the last drops in the glass before pouring another drink.

He was just taking his seat again when Stabb came in.

"We have visitors," Stabb said, smiling.

"I hope you have rolled out the red carpet," Vishinsky said.

Stabb picked up a remote control from the table and worked the buttons. A wooden panel at the end of the room slid open, opposite Vishinsky. "I thought we'd let them get a little bit farther. Not just to get their hopes up, but so there really is no chance of escape."

Behind the wooden panel was a large screen. It flickered into life as Stabb pressed another button. "I've had the security feed patched through," he said. "Magda is keeping an eye on things at security control, and she's sending the relevant pictures through to us here."

The grainy black-and-white image on the screen was clear enough. It showed a large storage container. Beside the container, something moved and the camera zoomed in to show a figure. As it turned, it was obviously Jade, her fair hair pale in the monochrome image, falling about her shoulders. She seemed to talk to someone out of sight behind the tank. Then, in a burst of speed, she was running around the tank.

The camera struggled to follow her. Then it let her go, moving back to its previous position.

"We want to make sure we have them both," Stabb said.

Sure enough, several moments later another figure appeared where the girl had been. A figure dressed in an identical coat, but with the hood pulled up so the face was in shadow. The figure was a similar size and shape, but for the moment that the face was clearly visible inside the hood of the coat, Stabb and Vishinsky could see that the hair was away from the face, apparently shorter.

"The boy as well," Vishinsky said. He took a gulp of vodka and slammed down the glass on the table in front of him. "Good. We have them. Take no chances, Mr. Stabb. These children have caused me enough trouble already. We know where they are now; take as many guards as you wish from wherever they are no longer needed."

Stabb nodded. "I'll send Magda to get them."

On the screen behind Stabb, the image changed to another camera. It showed Jade running across an open space. The image changed again—this time to show another point, just ahead of the previous one. The hooded figure appeared in the shot, making its wary way past a pipeline.

"They have no idea, do they?" Stabb said. "They don't even realize there are cameras. That they're starring in a film."

"It is not a film I have seen before," Vishinsky said. He rolled his glass in his hand, letting the last drops of the clear liquid coat the sides. "But I can guess exactly how it ends."

Chance lay on his mattress, staring up at the single naked bulb in the ceiling above, and listened to the sound of running feet and shouted orders. After a while it went quiet. Something was up, some commotion. Whatever it was, it was unlikely to be anything to do with him, Chance decided.

He changed his mind when he heard the scrape of the key turning in the lock. This could be his last chance, he decided—while many of the guards were busy. If he could get out of his prison, the storeroom, then maybe . . .

Chance was on his feet and across the small room, pressing himself to the wall behind the door as it started to open. He let it open wide enough for whoever was there to see the empty mattress. The door hesitated—and Chance grabbed it and wrenched it fully open, launching himself at the figure standing alone in the doorway.

He knocked the figure to the ground, landed astride it, raised his fist and prepared to bring it crashing down.

"Dad!" the figure beneath him yelled. It was Rich.

"What the hell are you doing?" Chance demanded in astonishment.

"Rescuing you. Sorry."

They both got to their feet. Rich was rubbing his ribs where Chance had landed on him.

"No, I'm sorry," Chance said. "You okay?"

"Just winded," Rich assured him. "There was a guard, but he went with lots of others just now. We need to get moving. Watch out for the camera, over there," he warned. "I've got a map with them marked. Lots of other useful stuff too. At least, I hope it's useful."

"Good man. I hope you're going to tell me your sister

had the good sense to stay at home," Chance said. Rich shrugged. "So where did the guards go—you arrange a diversion?"

"Yeah," Rich said, following Chance along a narrow walkway between two low concrete buildings. "Only there's a bit of a problem."

"What's that?" Chance checked the area at the end of the walkway and then they both ran quickly across.

"Jade is the diversion," Rich told him.

Stabb joined Magda beside a massive pipeline. Other pipes fed into it, through a complex arrangement of valves and taps.

"They are just about to come through there," Magda said, pointing to the gap between an enormous circular storage tank and a stack of pipes that rose like a wall. The gap emerged into an open area between more storage tanks, and guards were already in position with guns aimed, ready for the intruders to appear.

"I see you're ready for them," Stabb said.

Magda spoke quietly into her radio, pushing her long hair away from her ear. "I've sent guards into the other end of the passageway now, so they can't turn around, or go back, or run away. There really is no escape."

"Good. We don't want any nasty surprises at this stage."

Magda was listening to her radio. "I think our guests are about to arrive," she said.

Sure enough, a figure was emerging cautiously from the gap between tank and pipes. Its face was hidden beneath the raised hood of the bulky coat, but it obviously caught sight of the waiting guards—turned and ran.

A moment later, the figure was back, running out of the gap and into the open area. It skidded to a halt and stuck its hands up.

Behind the figure, half a dozen armed guards appeared from the gap.

Magda laughed. "Like a rat in a trap."

Stabb laughed too. But then, abruptly, he stopped. "Where's the other one?" he demanded. "Where's the girl?"

"They must have caught her already, in the passageway," Magda said. She led the way down to where the guards were still aiming their guns at the figure in the hooded coat. As she went she spoke again into her radio, her voice becoming more urgent and angry.

"That's impossible," Magda said to Stabb. "She was there. Security say they saw her clearly on the camera going in. But now—she isn't there."

Stabb strode up to the captured youngster. "Where is she?" he demanded. "Where's your sister?"

He reached out and pulled back the hood.

And Jade's blond hair spilled out of it around her shoulders. "Right here," she said. "Did you think there was someone else with me?"

On a metal walkway high above, stretched between storage tanks, John and Rich Chance looked down at the scene below. They could see the guards with their guns aimed, and they could see Magda and Stabb shouting at Jade.

"I know how they feel," Chance said.

"We can't just leave her," Rich told him.

"Of course not. We're going home. All of us. Together." Chance took the backpack from Rich and reached inside. "Just got a couple of things to sort out first."

23

"It was just you," Magda realized.

Despite the desperate situation, Jade was grinning. Her idea had worked perfectly. "Never saw the both of us together, did you?" She thrust her hands into her coat pockets. "You'll never find Rich now."

"You little bitch!" Magda shrieked. She lashed out, slapping Jade across the face.

It stung like hell, but Jade remained defiant. She was determined to stand up to the woman. "You're the one who hits like a girl," Jade said. In the pocket of her coat, she had found something—something she'd forgotten she had. She managed to ease open the top of the cigarette packet and felt inside.

Magda swung her arm back for another go. Her long black hair was in a whirl around her head as she moved.

And Jade brought the cigarette lighter out of her pocket, flicking the top of it as she reached out.

The scrape of flint. The pop of the ignition. A tiny spark of flame. Jade thrust the lighter into the swirl of Magda's long hair. And suddenly, the tiny flame was a mass of fire.

Magda screamed. Stabb watched in openmouthed amazement. The guards were frozen in a semicircle, staring as the flames raged through Magda's hair and down her back. She was screaming, clutching at her head, shaking it back and forth. Then she fell to the ground, rolling desperately as her clothes too caught fire.

Stabb pointed a gun at Jade. She stared down the black hole of the barrel. He grabbed her hand, the one holding the lighter, and stared at the small silver object clutched between her fingers. Stared at the engraved outline of a heart as it glinted in the flickering of the flames behind them.

"I've seen that before," he said. Despite the situation, he sounded elated, though Jade had no idea why. He ripped the lighter from her grasp.

From high above, Jade caught a glimpse of movement—something falling toward them. She saw the two figures on the gantry between the fuel tanks, and instinctively knew to look away from the falling shape.

Apparently sensing that she had seen something, Stabb glanced around, just as the flash grenade exploded. It was more light and sound than destructive power, but it robbed Stabb of his vision and scattered the guards.

Jade ran. She hoped that Rich and her father could see where she was going through the smoke and that they would find her, but she didn't have time to look back as the smoke billowed out from the point of impact. She sprinted back the way she had come, between the tanks and the pipes.

Through the drifting smoke, Rich could see two of the guards running to help Magda. They were using their jackets to beat out the flames and smother the fire.

Jade was running too, but Stabb was just standing there, staring at the lighter he had taken from Jade.

"What the hell did she do that for?" Chance said. He sounded angry and confused.

"Come on," Rich said. "Let's help her." He could recall the walkway they were on from his map of the installation. There should be a way down farther along, at the next storage tank. Then they'd be in the same area and could find Jade.

Chance had the backpack over his shoulder and was running with Rich.

"We'll get you another lighter," Rich gasped, breathless, as they ran.

"That's not the point," Chance told him. He eased Rich aside and went first down a metal ladder down the side of the tank that led to the ground close to where Jade had made her escape.

"Then what is the point?" Rich asked. "We came a long way to rescue you, not to get told off."

"And I came a long way to stop Vishinsky getting a sample of fuel that he needs—a sample I took from him and hid."

He reached the bottom of the ladder and stepped back so that Rich could join him.

"We know all about that," Rich said. "People keep on at us to tell them where it's hidden, though I don't know why it's so important. But I still don't see how—" Rich froze, one foot just short of the ground. "Your lighter," he realized. "The fuel sample was in your lighter."

"That's right. The fuel sample mixed with the lighter fluid—it works just like normal, so no one would ever know. Except that now Stabb has it. And, thanks to Jade, he knows it works."

Rich got out the map and together they examined it.

"Jade was running that way." Rich quickly traced the route she had taken. "We should be able to catch up with her here—assuming she's heading to where she came in." He pointed to the place where Jade had cut the wire before Rich had taken the cutters from her and made his way around to his own, different point of entry. "We'll have to be careful to avoid the cameras."

"No worries," Dad told him. He patted the backpack over his shoulder. "Little box of tricks in here, which I've turned on. It blanks out the cameras when we're within range. I set the range, so they're all out. Where did you get this stuff anyway?"

They were jogging between rows of massive metal pipes. "Friend of yours," Rich said. "I don't know his real name and he thinks you're called Harry."

Jade could hear the sound of booted feet coming after her. It wasn't far now—not far back to the hole she had cut in the fence. Hopefully, Rich would have realized where she was heading and would come to help. And Dad—he had rescued Dad. She'd seen them together on the gantry.

She turned a corner and found herself running between two low concrete buildings. Behind her, she could hear the guards gaining ground. She glanced back and saw the uniformed men turn the corner and start after her. At the far end of the buildings in front of her, two figures appeared. Jade slowed, then realized who they were. She sprinted as fast as she could toward Rich and her father.

At that moment a metal grille slid out from the side of one of the buildings in front of her. Another grille slid out from the other side of the passage to meet it.

Jade ran as fast as she could, but the grilles met and she slammed painfully into the mesh. It was too tightly woven to get a grip on or to climb.

"Jade!" Chance shouted as he skidded to a halt at the barriers. He tried to pry the metal gates apart, but they were firmly shut.

"The lighter," Rich said. "You have to get it back—it's the fuel sample they need. Jade!"

She was too exhausted, and too astonished, to answer. The first of the guards arrived and clamped a hand down on her shoulder. She shook it off angrily and glared up at the grinning man. Behind him, Stabb was walking slowly toward her along the passageway, and with him was Viktor Vishinsky. He was holding the lighter that Stabb had wrenched from her fingers just minutes before. The lighter that had seemed so unimportant . . .

"The perfect hiding place," Vishinksy said. He raised his voice to call through the mesh gates. "I congratulate you, Mr. Chance. A good choice. It still works as a lighter—who would ever guess?"

Vishinsky handed the lighter to one of the guards and gave him an order in Russian. The guard nodded and ran back down the passageway. "I shall have it analyzed and then we can make as much of the formula as we need. Thank you so very much."

"For what?" Jade demanded.

"It's fuel that's been treated with a special substance that Vishinsky can now duplicate," Chance said.

"You mean, like super-fuel?" Rich wondered.

Vishinsky smiled. He peered through the mesh at Rich and his father.

"Not quite," Vishinsky said. "The sample contained in that lighter is an antidote—something to reverse another process that I have been developing. You see, my scientists have developed a substance that acts like a virus, attacking oil and making any oil-based fuel useless."

"Why do you want to make a fuel that doesn't work?" Jade asked.

"Think of the havoc it will wreak once the infected fuel is introduced to the fuel supply. Cars and trucks will stop, perhaps in the middle of a highway. Planes will fall out of the sky. The transport system will simply collapse. No one will dare to use any fuel that might be contaminated—not when their very survival depends on it. Once I introduce the virus into a fuel line, it spreads rapidly. From this pumping station alone I could infect a large proportion of Europe's fuel."

"And the antidote in the lighter reverses the process, right?" Rich said, through the grille. "Makes it burn properly again—like normal fuel."

"Precisely," Vishinsky replied. "And this antidote that can treat the contaminated, useless fuel and make it work again—or protect uncontaminated fuel so it will survive the infection—"

"—will be worth a fortune," Rich interrupted. "When you infect all the oil supplies that pass through here, no one will know what fuel is safe to use and what's been infected. And then you can make a fortune offering to provide guaranteed safe supplies, which you've treated with this antibody."

Vishinsky turned to Chance. "Really, I must congratulate you on your children, Mr. Chance—or should that be your late wife?"

Jade lunged at Vishinsky, but a guard held her back.

"And what about all the people you kill with your contaminated fuel," Chance replied. "The cars that stop, the planes that drop out of the sky?"

"You have to create demand," Vishinsky told him, smiling. "That is the way you survive in business—and prosper. For too long Krejikistan has been just a link in a pipeline, a way station to somewhere else, but with this antidote we have a chance to make something of ourselves—to be more than just a lucky freak of geography. Our entire history has been defined by where we are, not who or what we are. The Mongols went right through Krejikistan—they didn't even think we were worth invading. At least under the Soviets, under Communism, we counted for something. Hard work could be seen as a purpose and goal in and of itself. But now?"

"You make money," Jade said. "The Russians pay for the use of your pipelines."

He gave a snort of derision. "Horses or pipelines, they all run right through and never care where they are going, who they are trampling on. They see us as an inconvenience, no more. An expense. Unless we prove them wrong, we will become as weak as those fools in the Kremlin have become, as decadent and soft and complacent as the West. Now is the time to stand up for ourselves, to achieve what we can. You wait—soon everyone will know about Krejikistan."

He clapped his hands together as if bringing a meeting to a close. "And now all that remains is to release my infection into the pipelines. When I am well away from here, naturally. Just in case there are any repercussions. Though I don't expect any."

"You don't think people will notice that the contaminated fuel came from your pumping station?" Chance said. "And that it all started appearing at the same time?"

"I don't think so, no. You see, I have a system set up all ready to inject my formula into the pipelines at a single central point. But I'm not injecting the raw substance. That would, as you point out, be rather too obvious. Oh, no, we will introduce slow-release capsules that dissolve and release the infection. All with different release times. It will seem truly random, believe me."

"And where will you be?" Rich asked.

"At my castle in the foothills, well away from here." Vishinsky reached out and brushed the back of his hand against Jade's cheek. She drew back and he smiled. "With your charming daughter."

"What makes you think I'd let you do that?" Chance asked.

Vishinsky laughed. "I was forgetting. How could you? When you are dead already." He turned to Stabb. "Give the order."

"What are you doing?" Jade yelled. "Stop—you've got me. You don't need them too!" She struggled out of the grip of the soldier who held her and launched herself at Stabb. He pushed her away, talking urgently into his radio. Jade fell to the ground, and two of the guards dragged her back to her feet.

Chance was shouting from the other side of the barrier. "What's going on? If you hurt her, Vishinsky, I'll kill you!"

"Jade—are you all right?" Rich was yelling.

Vishinsky's laughter increased. "Kill me? And how will you do that?" He turned away, gesturing to the guards holding Jade. Holding her tightly by the arms, they dragged her away.

She twisted and fought, but could not break free. Jade managed to look back—to see the silhouetted shapes of Rich and her dad against the mesh of the barrier. Then there was a rattle of machine-gun fire and the mesh was suddenly peppered with craters where the bullets had hit. Jade blinked the tears from her eyes, and when she could focus again, she saw that the silhouettes were gone.

24

Chance hurled Rich to one side before diving the other way himself. A split second later, bullets hammered into the mesh gate right where Rich had been standing.

The sound of gunfire was still echoing around the passageway as Chance leaped back to his feet and sprinted at the guard in front of them. The man was out of bullets, desperately trying to jam a new clip into his machine pistol. Behind him, another guard appeared.

Rich yelled, but Chance didn't seem to hear him. Shoulder down, he ran full tilt into the first guard, sending him flying backward into the guard who had just arrived. The second guard was firing. The bullets slammed into his comrade and the two of them fell in a twisted heap. Chance dropped to the ground as the second guard's shots went high. As soon as they stopped, Chance was up again—kicking at the guard as he yanked the gun from the man's hands.

In the sudden silence, Rich ran to join him beside the prone bodies of the guards. "What now?" he asked.

"Find somewhere to lay low for a bit. Then we get Jade back and sort out Vishinsky."

"Oh, right," Rich said. "Easy."

Stabb kept the gun aimed at Jade the whole time. She was pushed roughly into the back of Vishinsky's limousine. Jade couldn't help but smile as she thought of what had happened to his last car.

But her amusement was short-lived as Stabb and Vishinsky climbed in on either side of her, reminding Jade how much trouble she was in. She wondered what had happened to Rich and her dad, but there was nothing she could do except hope they were coping for themselves. If anyone could, it was those two, she decided. She had to stay positive.

Armed guards were piling into trucks and jeeps. It seemed like everyone was leaving the huge complex. Did that mean that Dad and Rich really were dead? How could she find out?

"Abandoning ship?" Jade asked Vishinsky.

"Not entirely," Vishinsky replied, smiling. "I shall leave a few guards, to keep up appearances. But it is as well to be cautious. And it may be necessary to make it appear that intruders broke in and sabotaged the systems and pipelines here."

"Which wouldn't be very plausible if there was a whole army on guard," Jade realized. "That's why you're leaving too—you might need an alibi."

"Unlikely, but possible," Vishinsky agreed. "You will like my castle in the foothills of the Carnovian Mountains. It used to be a frontier fort, guarding the pass from the Ukraine into our country. Whatever happens here, you will be very safe there, for your short stay."

"For your very short stay," Stabb added. Both he and Vishinsky laughed.

The few guards that were left at the complex were patrolling at ground level. Up on the high walkways between the storage tanks, Rich and Chance had seen the convoy of vehicles, led by Vishinsky's limousine, puling out of the main gates and leaving the facility.

"Doesn't want to be found near the scene of the crime," Chance said.

"You think he's got Jade with him?" Rich asked.

"I should think so. Don't worry—we'll get her back."

They consulted the map and worked out the next part of their route. "We need to get to this point, the main pumping systems," Chance said. "That's where the main pipelines converge."

"So it's the obvious point for Vishinsky to contaminate all the oil supplies as they go through."

"Exactly."

To get to the main pumping facility, they had to descend to ground level and cross a wide roadway that ran through the center of the site. There were still several guards patrolling it. Chance and Rich hid in the shadows of a long block of offices and watched the armed guards walking slowly up and down the roadway.

"Do we have any more of those smoke grenades?" Rich asked.

"Just one. I'm saving that." Chance smiled. "Never know when the occasion might need it. Anyway, we don't want to attract attention; that'll bring them all running." He hefted the machine pistol slung over his shoulder, and Rich knew that if he had to use it, he would. "They all seem to think we're either dead or someone else's problem. Let's keep it that way."

They worked their way to a point at the end of the road, close to the perimeter fence. There was just one guard there, out of sight of his fellows.

"Doubt they'll miss him for a while," Chance said. "Go and have a word."

"Delighted." Rich grinned and stepped out from the cover of a storage tank into plain sight. The guard did not see him at first, so Rich waved.

The guard looked at him warily and raised his gun. Rich waved again, still grinning.

"Okay, you got me," he called. "I can't hide forever. Come on, slap on the handcuffs."

Gun still aimed at Rich, the guard came closer. He pulled a radio from his pocket and raised it slowly to speak.

But before he got the opportunity, Chance exploded from cover farther down the road and ran at the guard, who turned in astonishment. He saw Chance and panicked, dropping his radio and his gun. A moment later, Chance's fist slammed into him, and the guard dropped like a brick to the roadway.

Rich dragged the guard by his feet out of sight, and then he and Chance made their way to the pumping station. It was like an enormous aircraft hangar, with pipes and cables converging on it from all over the site. The entrance was a pair of huge double doors, which stood open, and Rich could see several oil tankers inside. He and Chance walked slowly and cautiously past the big trucks and behind them found a mass of pipes and valves that came together like an intricate metal Christmas tree. The whole thing was humming and vibrating as oil flowed through various pipes and valves.

"It's all automated," Chance explained. "Controlled by computer, so that the right amount of oil from the right pipelines gets fed into the correct systems in the correct quantities on schedule."

"And this is where Vishinsky will contaminate the oil?"

"Somewhere here. Goodness only knows where, though. Any of these pipes could be ready to feed contaminated fuel into the whole system."

"So how do we stop it?" Rich asked.

"We can't. Not until we know Jade is safe."

Rich thought about this. "Are you saying we have to go and rescue Jade, then come back and stop it?"

"I doubt there will be time. First hint of trouble and Vishinsky will release the contaminated fuel. He's only waiting now to be sure he's well out of it."

"So what's the plan?"

Chance was rummaging through the backpack. He produced a black box with a switch and display on it—something that Rich had wondered about.

"Normally, I'd use this," Chance explained. "Strap it to the right valve or pipeline, and when it's set, it detects vibration. Sets off a small explosive charge. Enough to rupture the pipe and ignite the fuel inside."

Rich whistled. "Quite a bang."

"Enough to blow up this whole place. There are safety measures—cutouts and shutters and stuff—to stop the blast spreading down the pipelines. But it would certainly destroy Vishinsky's contaminated fuel stocks here. Only problem is . . ." He walked over to the massive arrangement of pipes and put his hand on one. "Feel that."

Rich joined him and placed his own hand on the pipe. He could feel it trembling and shaking. "It's vibrating already."

"I hoped we could attach it to Vishinsky's contaminated fuel and it would go off when he started to transfer it into the systems. But we don't know which pipe we need, and there's so much fuel going through so many of the pipes already, the thing would just blow at once. We need some way to set it off ourselves."

"Preferably when we're not here," Rich pointed out. He took out the cell phone that Ralph had given him. "Maybe your friend Ralph will be able to help out?"

Chance took the phone from him. "Rich," he said, "you're a genius. But it isn't Ralph who's going to blow this place to kingdom come. Now all we need is some way of getting into Vishinsky's fortress. I doubt the subtle approach will work."

"What about one of them?" Rich pointed to the oil tankers parked close by.

Chance considered, then said, "I don't think one of these will do it. We'd need something much tougher, heavier, more robust. Any other suggestions?" He turned back toward the pipelines, obviously not expecting to get a reply.

"What about a tank?" Rich asked.

In the central fortified building of the old frontier fort, Viktor Vishinsky rubbed his hands together with satisfaction. The room was his control center, with computer connections to his vast business empire all over the world.

A bank of monitors almost filled one wall—incongruous

against the rough stonework behind them. Several showed graphic diagrams of the pumping systems at the main facility. One was a view of the whole complex from a security camera on the perimeter. Another showed a view of the main gate of the castle itself, then of an empty stairwell, followed by guards patrolling the ancient battlements, the monitors constantly changing as they switched between different cameras.

Jade was standing at the back of the room, watching. Stabb was right beside her. He wasn't pointing a gun at her anymore, but there were enough armed guards around the place to ensure that Jade had no chance of escape. As everything had gone to Vishinsky's plan, she had no doubt he would have her killed. She had been staring at the image of the main KOS installation on the screen, looking for any sign that Dad and Rich were there, but apart from a single oil tanker driving away from the facility, there was little sign of life.

A technician sitting at the bank of monitors turned to talk to Vishinsky, who nodded with evident delight.

"Everything is ready," Vishinsky called across to Stabb and Jade. "In a few moments, we can begin the computer sequence that will release our contaminated oil into the pipeline system. And within hours it will be flowing through Europe. No one will know where it came from or where it has got to. Not until they realize their precious fuel doesn't work or is . . . unstable. Nothing can stop it now."

"Dad'll stop you," Jade retorted. "You haven't won yet."

"Daddy coming to help?" Stabb said. "From beyond the grave?"

"Even if by some miracle he is still alive, there is nothing he can do," Vishinsky assured Jade.

One of the guards hurried up to Stabb and spoke to him quickly in Russian. Jade had no idea what he said, but Stabb ran over to the monitor controls and worked them furiously.

"And nothing you can do either. You may have put Magda in the hospital, but you are all alone now," Vishinsky was saying. "No one can help you. No one is coming to your rescue."

"You might want to look at this," Stabb said. He sounded suddenly nervous. The screen above him changed from a shot of the inside of the fortress's courtyard to a view from the main gate. A narrow road curled through the foothills of the mountains, down from the fortress into the valley below, and rumbling inexorably up the road, heading straight for the main gate, was a large tank.

Jade almost cried out in triumph. Her eyes filling with tears of joy, she saw the turret swivel and the gun lift—to point right at the camera. There was a brilliant flash and the screen went blank.

At the same moment, the whole room shook as the shell impacted on the ancient gatehouse. The lights flickered and dust fell from the ceiling. Several of the monitors blanked out. Stabb was shouting, waving guards from the room.

One of the blanked screens flickered back to life—to show the dented and damaged tank in the main gateway into the fortress. It was covered with stone blocks and rubble that had fallen across it when the gatehouse collapsed. It didn't look like it would move again, but the hatch on the turret was open.

From outside came the sound of machine-gun fire.

Rich was running across the uneven paving slabs of the main courtyard of the castle. He had a job to do. He had to get to Jade. Chance was drawing the fire of the guards, leading them away from the main keep, where Ralph had said Vishinsky had his control center.

The way was clear, but Rich had to negotiate rubble from the damage caused by the tank's shell as well as drifting smoke from the last grenade. He saw the dark shapes of guards stumbling past him in the gloom, and hoped he was still heading the right way.

Sure enough, he found the steps up into the keep—the metal doors standing open. Inside, there was a small antechamber and then he was standing at the back of the control center. Everyone's attention seemed to be on the screens at the far end of the room. One showed a view of the oil facility Rich and Dad had so recently escaped from. Most of the others now showed views from the security cameras in the fortress. On one of them, Rich saw his dad run past—then pause, turn and fire straight at the camera.

As the screen went black, there was a cry of elation from nearby and Rich saw Jade. She was not ten yards from him. He edged closer.

And the cold metal of a gun barrel jammed into his cheek.

"Looking for me?" Stabb asked.

Vishinsky stood in front of the monitors. He regarded Rich and Jade with undisguised contempt.

"I should have you both shot now," he said. "My only regret is that your father won't witness it."

"He'll surrender, if he knows you have us. If you promise to let us go," Rich said. "You could call him on his cell. That's how I'm supposed to let him know we're safe. But he probably wouldn't believe you." He turned and winked at Jade, hoping she'd realize he knew what he was doing. Hoping Vishinsky or Stabb wouldn't see.

Vishinsky was looking at them both through narrowed eyes. "Oh, the pleasure of it," he said quietly. "The pleasure of letting him hear you die." From outside came the rattle of more gunfire and then an explosion. It sounded closer now.

Vishinsky took out his cell phone and flipped it open. "Mr. Stabb, start the process."

Another explosion—right outside.

Stabb pressed a button on the main console and a monitor screen above displayed a large 20.

Twenty minutes maybe? But Rich's hopes were dashed as the 20 became 19. Then 18 . . .

"What's the telephone number?" Vishinsky demanded.

17 . . .

Jade shook her head. "Don't tell him, Rich."

16 . . .

"Tell me, or Mr. Stabb will shoot your sister in the leg," Vishinsky said.

15 . . .

"Tell me, and it will be quick for her at least," he added.

14 . . .

"I promise."

13 . . .

"Rich, please . . ." Jade said. "Don't . . ."

12 . . .

Rich squeezed her hand.

11 . . .

And told Vishinsky the phone number.

10 . . .

Vishinsky punched it into his cell.

9 . . .

Outside, the gunfire was closer still. Someone screamed.

8 . . .

Vishinsky put the phone to his ear.

7 . . .

He was smiling.

6 . . .

"Mr. Stabb," Vishinsky said. "I'll tell you when." He gestured at Rich and Jade standing in front of him.

5 . . .

Rich could hear the phone connect—even above the gunfire, he could hear the rhythmic sound of the ring tone.

4 . . .

Stabb's gun was pointed straight at Rich as the countdown reached:

3 . . .

25

"No answer," Vishinsky said. "Not yet."

"He won't ever answer," Jade said.

The countdown was on 2.

"She's right," Rich said calmly.

1.

"You see, that wasn't Dad's phone number."

Stabb's cry of alarm drew Vishinsky's attention back to the monitors. It was not clear if the man even heard what Rich was saying.

"It's the number of a phone I was given," Rich was saying. "Dad and I left it in your pumping station, attached to an explosive that can detect the slightest movement. Set to vibrate."

On the monitor an inferno raged through the KOS pumping station. A silent ball of flame engulfed the central buildings. The screens went dead.

Vishinsky and Stabb ran to the window. In the distance, the sky glowed an unnatural orange as oil storage tanks exploded one after another in a chain of fire around the pumping station.

"By calling that number," Rich said, "you set the bomb off."

"The pipelines are shutting down," Stabb shouted above the noise and confusion. He looked at Vishinsky. "The safety measures are engaging. There's no way your oil can get through now—even if any of it escaped that blast."

The noise was getting louder. A steady *thwock-thwock* of sound from outside, like a swarm of giant insects attacking. Stabb was frantically changing views on the monitors. Most of them were full of smoke and fire. Finally, he found a clearer view across the top of the fortress. He glanced at it and swore. He looked at Rich, turned and ran from the room.

"Stabb!" Vishinsky shouted after him. "Stabb—where are you going?"

Vishinsky dashed to the monitor. The image on the screen zoomed in on dark shapes in the distance—helicopters.

"Expecting guests?" Rich asked Vishinsky.

The man did not reply. He reached into his jacket and started to pull out a pistol, but before he managed it, Jade kicked out, catching him in the stomach. He doubled up in pain and Rich punched him in the face. The pistol went flying, well out of reach.

"Come on," Rich said. He grabbed Jade's hand and they turned toward the doors. Before they got there, Vishinsky barreled into them, knocking them both off their feet. With a roar, he swept up a gun from the ground close by and brought it around. He stood between the children and the doors now, aiming at them with the machine pistol.

"You may have delayed my plans," he snarled, "but now you're going to pay for it." His finger tightened on the trigger.

He barely had time to register what hit him. The solid mass of an ex-SAS soldier smashed into Vishinsky from behind, sending him staggering and skidding forward.

"Cavalry's arriving," Chance announced.

Jade and Rich dived to the ground as Vishinsky fired. The shots rattled over their heads. Jade leaped back up and jumped at Vishinsky. She connected with both feet together—slamming into him and sending him flying. As Vishinsky staggered backward, Rich grabbed his leg and yanked it hard.

Vishinsky stumbled, gun still firing. The bullets hammered into the monitor screens and control desk. Screens exploded and cables hissed and spat. Vishinsky fell onto the console with a cry.

The gun fell to the ground and Vishinsky's back arched as the live cables severed by his shots connected. His whole body was bathed in a pale blue light for a moment. Then he collapsed back into an explosion of sparks and flame and was still.

"All good things come to an end," Chance said. "And bad ones too, it seems."

They ran to the window to see three black helicopters hovering over the fortress courtyard. Dark-clad figures were dropping rapidly on ropes to the ground. The air was split with the renewed sound of gunfire.

As Rich, Jade and Chance stepped from the main control room out into the antechamber beyond, the doors behind them were pushed shut.

"Hold it there," Stabb said. "Turn around, slowly."

Chance sighed. "Ready?" he breathed.

Rich and Jade both nodded.

Then they turned, slowly, to face Stabb. He was standing several feet away from them, a handgun aimed at Chance. "You're going to get me out of here," he said.

"No," Chance told him. "We're leaving now." He turned slowly away again.

Eyes wide, Stabb stepped forward, thrusting the gun into Chance's back. "Look at me!" he yelled.

But his attention was all on Chance. He didn't see Jade's foot swinging up at the gun. Didn't notice Rich's punch coming at him.

Both connected. The gun clattered across the floor. Stabb gave a cry of surprise, which became a grunt of pain as Rich's fist slammed into his stomach. He doubled over—right into the upper-cut punch Chance delivered to the man's chin as he turned back. Stabb collapsed backward, hitting the stone floor hard. A low moan escaped from his lips and he was still.

Chance leaned down and pulled something from the unconscious man's breast pocket. A silver lighter.

"That's mine, I believe," he said quietly.

26

The sound of the shooting and explosions from out-side was almost gone now. It was replaced by the sound of someone chuckling.

It was Ardman. He had one arm in a sling, and a bandage across one side of his forehead. Beyond him, Rich and Jade could see figures in dark camouflage moving quickly through the ruins of the fortress, rounding up Vishinsky's surviving guards.

"I was hoping to be of some assistance," Ardman said.

"But you seem to have everything pretty much under control. And my people tell me you've not left them very much to do out there." He nodded in the direction of the castle courtyard.

"Well, if you will insist on arriving just after the nick of time," Chance told him, grinning.

"Anything for an old friend. Oh—and Mr. Halford sends his regards. I've sent some people to collect him and take him home. It seems he forgot to bring his passport and there might be some formalities that need attending to."

"All well within your capabilities, I'm sure," Chance said. "Can I assume you three know each other?"

"We've met," Jade said as Ardman led them out of the keep and across to where a helicopter was standing on one of the few level areas left inside the fortress walls.

"We had tea together at the Clarendorf," Rich said.

"It got a bit busy, so we didn't have time to leave a tip," Jade said.

"I expect Ardman did," Chance said. "Whatever the circumstances."

Ardman stood by the helicopter. He looked at the three of them with amusement.

"So," Ardman said, "apart from arranging for some suitable education, a spot of well-deserved leave and a safe journey home, is there anything else I can get you?"

Chance looked at Jade and Rich. Rich and Jade looked at their dad.

John Chance grinned, and pulled Rich and Jade into a hug beside the waiting helicopter.

"No thanks," Chance told Ardman as he held his children tight. "I've got everything I need."

Turn the page for a preview of

DEATH RUN

Jack Higgins's next novel with Justin Richards

It was hot and humid in Venice in the last week of August. One canal looked pretty much like another to Jade, the churches all looked the same and the whole place smelled old and damp. It was probably better than hanging around in London with nothing to do till school started again, but if she had to eat any more pasta or gelato, Jade reckoned there would be serious trouble.

As usual, it was difficult to know what Dad thought of it all. But since he'd brought them here, he was presumably enjoying himself. They stayed in a small family run hotel close to the Grand Canal. It amused Jade that the bar closed at nine in the evening and if Dad wanted a drink after that, he had to find the night porter.

Rich seemed to be enjoying himself. He greeted every new street or stretch of water, every café and old building with excitement. "Have you seen this?" he exclaimed with interest as they turned into a small square close to the canal.

"Oh yeah, look," Jade muttered back. "Another church.

Well, who'd have thought." But she had to smile at his enthusiasm.

"Yeah, but they're all different," Rich told her. "I mean, talk about paintings!"

"You do that a lot," she pointed out.

"Only takes a few minutes to look around," Dad said. "We should do it while we're here."

"I suppose."

There was a small café opposite. Dad suggested they take a look in the church, then stop for a drink.

She didn't like to admit it, but Jade found it refreshingly cool inside the church. There were indeed paintings—several small icons and an ornamental screen. The paintings were dark with age, but Rich was fascinated.

"Are we having fun yet?" Dad said quietly to Jade.

"I suppose," she admitted.

"I'll take that as a yes, then." He smiled at her, and she couldn't help but smile back.

"It's fine, Dad. Great. Church, paintings, everything." Jade's smile widened into a grin. "Can we go now?"

They were getting toward the end of their stay in Venice, and Jade had found herself relaxing into the slow pace of the holiday. Perhaps she was adapting to the ways of the city. Or perhaps it was the heat. But by their last couple of days, Jade was as happy as her brother and father to sit outside the small café and let the day go by.

"I think that woman is following us," Rich said quietly as

he drank his Coke. Jade had ordered mineral water, while Dad had an espresso that was thick as syrup.

"Describe her," Dad said at once, not looking around. Jade glanced where Rich was looking, then away again, pretending to be admiring the small square they were in. It was just like a hundred other small squares they'd been to.

"Tall, slim. Smartly dressed. Long hair that's a sort of auburn color. I'm sure the same woman was a couple of tables away from us at dinner last night."

Dad frowned. "Sounds like a woman I noticed the other day in the casino."

"So you *were* in the casino?" Jade said.

"I mean the hotel. At the casino. I told you—I heard the alarms and nipped down to see what was happening."

"Climbing out the window and down the wall?" Jade pointed out.

Dad shrugged. "Force of habit. Anyway, it was a lot of fuss about nothing. False alarm or something. And it's probably a completely different woman. Just a coincidence."

"What if it isn't?" Rich asked. "What if she's . . . I don't know, an agent or something?"

Jade laughed at that. "More likely she's a tourist. If we go to the obvious boring touristy places, we're going to see some of the same obvious boring tourists, aren't we?"

Dad drained his coffee and pushed a few euros under the saucer to pay the bill. "Easy enough to find out."

"So what's the plan?" Jade asked.

"Well, you're complaining you're bored, Jade—what do you want to do for the rest of the afternoon?" Chance asked.

"Not churches," Jade said at once. "There was that little street of decent shops you wouldn't let us stop at yesterday."

"Because we're here on holiday, not to buy new sneakers and T-shirts," Rich reminded them.

"Okay," Dad said. "And you, Rich?"

"I'm happy to wander. Browse the shops a bit. Are we splitting up?"

Dad nodded. "We'll see if that woman follows any of us. I'll go first and double back around so I can follow her."

"Sneaky," Rich said. "But what if she follows you?"

"She won't. She won't realize I'm leaving." As he spoke, Dad stood up. "Meet back here in an hour, okay?"

"Okay," they both agreed.

Dad walked slowly, almost lazily into the café. Jade risked another quick look at the woman. She was reading a book, maybe a guidebook—a small paperback. She didn't seem to have reacted to Dad leaving the table. But then she was probably expecting him to come back and for all three of them to leave together.

"You really think she's following us?" Jade asked.

Rich shrugged. "We'll soon know."

Jade grinned. "If she is, I reckon it's just because she fancies Dad."

Rich shuddered at the thought. "That's so gross."

They stood up together, then headed off in opposite directions out of the little square. If the woman with the auburn hair noticed, she gave no sign.

After ten minutes, Rich was bored of wandering around on his own. He considered returning to the café, but that might spoil whatever Dad was up to. So instead he went looking for Jade. He remembered the street where she'd wanted to look at the designer clothes and sports stuff.

It was only a few minutes' walk. Rich paused on a steep-backed, narrow bridge over a canal and admired the view. He liked the way the water and the streets seemed to exist in harmony. The tall, square buildings emerging from the water made everything seem even more narrow and closed in.

He found Jade in the second shop he tried. She was trying on running shoes but hadn't found any she liked. Jade was picky when it came to running shoes. Actually, Rich thought, she was picky about most things.

"Find any good churches, then?" Jade asked as they walked slowly back along the street.

Rich shook his head. "Nothing worth mentioning."

"There's some weird stuff here," Jade said. She paused outside what seemed to be an antiques shop. "I mean, look at all that."

There were several chess sets in the window, laid out on marble boards. One of them was made of gold, and the tag hanging from the side of the board looked more like a telephone number than a price. On each side of the window display stood a figure, as if they were keeping guard. One was a woman in a brightly colored, flowing dress. The mannequin's face was a smooth, white mask with a peacock painted on it in brilliant blue. Dark holes for the eyes formed part of the feathers of the peacock.

"That's beautiful," Jade said in surprise.

"That isn't," said Rich, pointing at the other figure. "It's grotesque."

The second figure was a man. He wore long, dark robes and held a stick as if it was a magic wand. His face too was a mask—but a plain, gray mask that jutted out like an enormous cruel beak. The only color in the mask was the black outline of a pair of spectacles around the eyes.

"Who are they supposed to be?" Jade wondered.

"I don't know, but I wouldn't want to meet them outside of a shop display."

2

Once inside the café, John Chance asked if there was a back way out. There was, out past the waste bins and down a tiny alleyway alongside a canal. He made his way rapidly, ignoring the smell from the bins, and emerged into a side street just off the back of the square.

It took him only a minute to double back and approach the square from a different direction. He hesitated at the edge of the square, looking for the young woman Rich had described. He had taken a moment to case her out from inside the café— and it was definitely the woman he had noticed at the casino. A coincidence? It was possible, but highly unlikely. So who was she, and why was she following him?

But the table where the woman had been was empty. He would not get the answer to his questions just yet. Chance walked slowly around the square, looking along each of the streets leading off it in turn. There was no sign of the woman with auburn hair. Satisfied that, for now at least, he was not being watched, Chance returned to the table outside the café.

He'd had enough coffee for today, so he ordered a carafe of white wine.

He was halfway through it when Rich and Jade returned.

"So?" Jade asked as she sat down. She glanced disapprovingly at the wine. It was barely lunchtime and he'd started already. Still, at least he wasn't smoking.

"Yeah, what happened to your girlfriend?" Rich asked.

Dad took a pack of cigarettes out of his shirt pocket. "She didn't wait for me to introduce myself. I wondered if she'd followed either of you?"

"Not that we noticed," Jade said. "You're not going to smoke that, are you?" She was glaring at the cigarette between Dad's fingers.

"No, I'm going to juggle with it."

"Funny man."

Dad pushed the cigarette back into the pack. He was getting better, Jade had to admit. He did actually seem to listen to what she and Rich said. That was a distinct improvement.

"Speaking of jugglers," Dad was saying. "What's with the fancy dress party?"

Rich gasped, and Jade turned quickly to see what he and Dad were looking at.

It was like the shop display had come to life and followed them. A small group of half a dozen men was walking slowly into the little square from one of the side streets. They were all wearing dark business suits, and all had their faces covered by masks. The man at the front was wearing a savagely beaked gray face—just like in the display.

Behind him came two men in golden gargoyle masks, then a man whose face was completely white except for a single black teardrop on one cheek. Another of them was Harlequin—like the joker from a deck of cards, a black and red face with spikes springing from his head.

The last man wore the blank-eyed grinning face of a skull. Jade shuddered. If this was someone's idea of fun, it was pretty bizarre. And why wear heavy, dark clothes in this heat?

"Some sort of parade," Dad said. "Wrong time of year for Carnival."

Rich looked at Jade, and she saw how pale he was. "I don't like this."

"Me neither," she agreed. At first she'd thought, like Dad, that it was a bit of fun. Some sort of parade. Now Jade was sure it wasn't. There was something sinister about the figures—about the way they moved, the way they had paused just inside the square. They slowly swung around, as if looking for something. Or someone. They all stopped at the same point—staring directly at Jade, Rich and their father.

Dad's chair scraped backward on the flagstones as he stood up. "Wait for me back at the hotel."

"What are you going to do?" Jade asked.

"I don't know. Get moving."

"We can't leave you," Rich said. The men were walking

slowly across the square toward them. The beak of the gray mask was aimed directly at Dad.

"Move it!" Dad urged. "And don't worry. I'll probably overtake you."

Jade grabbed Rich's hand and together they ran from the square.

"We can't leave him with them," Rich gasped as they ran.

"What do you suggest?"

"We have to see what's happening." Rich slowed to a jog and Jade eased up as well. "We should go back."

"That's probably what they want."

"So what—do nothing?"

"No." Jade pointed to a small alleyway between two buildings. "If we cut through there, we can get back to the square on a different street. They won't expect that."

"You hope."

"All right, Einstein—let's hear your idea."

Rich sighed. "Let's try the alley," he conceded.

Dad was talking to the man in the gray, beaked mask. He was shaking his head, turning away. Then the masked man said something that Jade and Rich couldn't hear, but they heard their father laugh. He waved a hand as if dismissing whatever the masked man had said. Then he held up a finger—a "back in a minute" gesture—and walked into the café.

"He's all right," Jade realized. "He'll leg it out the back, like before."

"If they fall for it."

It didn't look like they had. The gray-masked man was gesturing to the two golden gargoyles, who ran after Dad into the café. Moments later there were shouts from inside and the other masked men followed in a hurry.

"I expect he'll be all right," Jade said.

"Course he will." Rich sounded more confident than Jade felt. "Think we should help him?"

"How? Come on, let's get back to the hotel like Dad said."

"And hope he meets us there."

It wasn't far, and walking briskly, they were back in half an hour. It probably wasn't the quickest route—Rich had led them back the same way as they had come that morning. At least they didn't stop at every church this time.

"You wait here," Rich told Jade as they walked through the little foyer into the small lounge bar. "I'll check he's not already back in his room. Anyone who knows the way could be here before us."

Jade slumped down on a sofa. It wasn't as comfortable as it looked, but she settled into it and watched the door. A large black car bumped up the narrow cobbled street outside and stopped opposite the hotel. No one got out, and Jade frowned. It was unusual to see a car right in the heart of Venice. For one thing, the streets weren't really wide enough. She was about to run up the stairs after Rich when she heard his scream.

Rich took the stairs two at a time. The door to their room was standing open, and he sighed with relief. He went straight in, not thinking it might be a trap.

As soon as he was through the door, everything went black. He had time to cry out in surprise and alarm—just once. Then he was fighting against the blanket that was tight over his face and shoulders. Rich was being dragged out of the room and back down the stairs. His feet caught on the threadbare carpet and knocked painfully against the wall of the stairwell as he was bundled away.

Soon he was on level ground again, the thin lounge carpet under his feet. Then he heard his feet scrape on the bare stone floor of the lobby, followed by the warm breeze on his hands and a brightness even through the blanket. He was struggling to speak, but his throat was clogged with dust and whenever he tried, he ended up coughing and choking. There were uneven cobbles under his feet now. His head was pushed roughly down and he was shoved forward—landing on something soft. A chair? Where was he?

An engine revved. A door slammed. Rich was in a car, and it was pulling away.

Jade emerged from behind the sofa. She'd been ready to fight the men to get Rich free. But a glance from her hiding place at the four men in Carnival masks had been enough to tell her it was no use. She'd end up being captured herself. It made her sick to her stomach, but the best option was to leave Rich to fend for himself.

At least he wouldn't be on his own—Jade would follow. But then she saw Rich bundled into the car opposite the hotel and her heart sank still lower. She couldn't follow a car.

But she'd try. She wouldn't give up and abandon her brother. Jade was out of the hotel and running after the car as it started up the street. She kept to the shadowed side of the pavement, hoping they wouldn't spot her. Mercifully, the dark limousine was going quite slowly up the uneven street. And Jade ran every day. If it kept to this speed, she might—just might—keep it in sight.

The car reached the end of the street and turned right. Almost immediately it turned again—toward the main street. Jade hesitated. Should she follow, or should she take a risk? She'd lose the car if she just followed. She'd risk it, she decided—take a shortcut she'd discovered along an alley and over a little canal bridge. That would bring her to the same junction as the car was making for. *Probably* making for . . .

At the junction, Jade paused for breath. There was no sign of the car. It couldn't have got here already. But after almost a minute, Jade realized it wasn't coming. It was too distinctive for her to have missed. She'd gambled and lost. The car had not been heading for the main road at all.

With a shout of frustration, Jade turned and kicked the wall of the building behind her.